Voyage

to

Silvermight

Dedication

David:
My Son Jasiah, the True Dragonsbane

Charlie:
My Wonderful Grandmothers

Special thanks from the co-authors to J.R.R. Tolkien for establishing the modern fantasy genre. His works are an inspiration.

This book is fiction. The people, places, events, and sand-swimming lobsterpods depicted within are fictitious. Any resemblance to persons living or dead or to real life places is purely coincidence and, in all honesty, probably a little disturbing.

ISBN 0-9728461-3-1

Printed in the U.S.A.

First Printing, May 2004

Voyage to Silvermight
Table of Contents

Fantasy Name Guide
for
Voyage to Silvermight

In fantasy books like Knightscares, some character names will be familiar to you. Some will not. To help you pronounce the tough ones, here's a handy guide to the unusual names found in
The Dragonsbane Horn: Voyage to Silvermight.

Amalgamoth
Uh - mal - gah - moth

Efreet
Eh - freet

Jasiah
Jay - sigh - uh

Kadze
Cod - zay

Mirelda
Muh - rell - duh

Shaddim
Shah - dim

Shelolth
She - lolth

Wyvern
Why - vern

The Sandy Sea

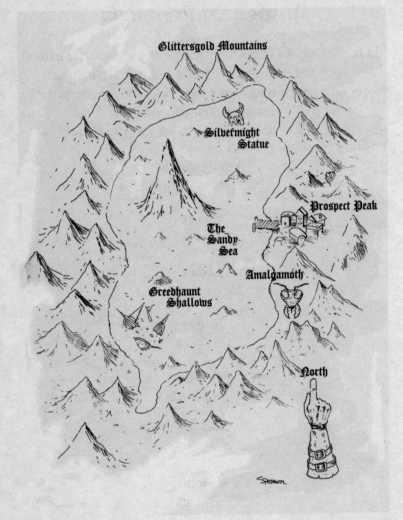

Glittersgold Mountains

Silvermight Statue

Prospect Peak

The Sandy Sea

Amalgamoth

Greedhaunt Shallows

North

Tiller's Field and Surroundings

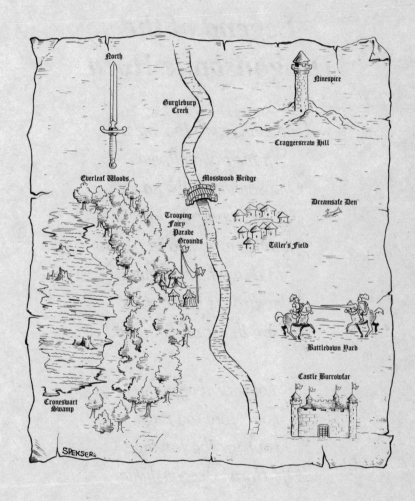

Legend of the Dragonsbane Horn

One waits with the wizard
In his hollow tome.
One sounds in the sands
Of the dwarven home.
One rings wrapped in roots
In damp forest loam.
One drones in the dark
Where the shaddim roam.

Four for the future.
Four 'fore the reign.
Four for the forging.
Of Horn Dragonsbane.

The Dragonsbane Horn
#1:
Voyage to Silvermight

David Anthony
and
Charles David

Hunted

1

I saw them when I closed my eyes. Their dark shapes blacker than night. Their fiery yellow eyes blazing like comets. They were coming for me.

Searching…

Hunting…

Their damp, stale breath tickled the back of my neck like a chilly breeze shivering through a graveyard. It smelled of dead leaves, wet soil, and worms.

They would catch me, and I knew their name.

Shaddim.

Shadows of night, groaning ghosts. They were coming for me.

"Just one more hour, lads."

Uncle Arick's deep voice interrupted my thoughts, and I blinked in the fading light of dusk.

It was getting dark, but I could see just fine. Darkness

didn't bother me. Even in the tiniest bit of starlight, my eyes saw almost as well as they did at noon.

It was nighttime that worried me. Night and what it brought with it. Shaddim prowled when the sun went down, slinking like thieves between shadows. They'd catch me if we didn't reach Tiller's Field soon.

"Will your backside hold out, Jasiah?" Uncle Arick asked, turning to grin at me.

Seated ahead of me, Kadze chuckled at my uncle's joke. He and I rode a few yards behind my uncle, sharing a horse and saddle. The seating didn't make for the most comfortable ride. Worrying about shaddim didn't help.

I wasn't a good rider, but our horse Chet was patient and calm. The last thing I needed was someone reminding me of how sore my backside should be from bouncing in a saddle.

"Aye, we're fine, Mr. Dragonsbane," Kadze said to my uncle. "*Even rolling downhill, a round stone will bump and bounce.*"

Hearing that, I couldn't keep from groaning. Kadze talked in riddles a lot. He called them *proverbs* and claimed they were very old and full of wisdom.

I scrunched up my face and scowled. *That's what you think*, I grumped at the back of his bald head. *The shaddim aren't hunting you.*

That was the problem. To Uncle Arick and Kadze, we were just traveling along Wagonwheel Road in the evening.

They didn't worry about shaddim the way I did. They didn't *feel* the monsters coming.

We were on our way to see the famous Wizard Ast. He had a very important quest to tell us about. Kids like Kadze and me had been summoned from all over the kingdom to meet with the wizard.

The quest had something to do with a magical instrument called the Dragonsbane Horn. When blown, the Horn would hypnotize every dragon that heard the sound. It was old, powerful, and dangerous.

My name is Dragonsbane, too. Jasiah Dragonsbane. But I'm not old, powerful, or dangerous. I'm an eleven year old boy with brown hair and brown eyes. I'm short and I don't look any older than nine.

Except for being able to see in the dark and hear a cat's tail swishing from across a room, I'm a pretty regular kid. Definitely not someone who'd go on a quest like a hero. I can't use a sword, cast spells, or fire a bow.

That's why it didn't make sense for the shaddim to be after me. I wasn't a threat. Why did they want me?

Ooowhooo-ooh-ooo.

A ghostly moan slithered in from the darkness, coming from everywhere at once. The creepy noise prickled the hairs on the back of my neck.

Uncle Arick immediately threw up a big hand. "Halt!" he hissed between clenched teeth as the dreadful moan came again.

Kadze pulled up rein and slid silently from the saddle. "*No*—" I started but the word died on my lips.

Ooowhooo-ooh-ooo.

A pack of shaddim appeared, floating just above the ground. They materialized from the darkness like ghosts. There were at least twenty of them.

We were surrounded.

For an instant, I froze with fear. My limbs trembled and my eyes stared, watching in terror as the black creatures glided closer. Then finally, I found my voice.

"Shaddim!" I cried too late.

The shaddim weren't hunting anymore. They'd found me.

2

"Get behind me!" Uncle Arick roared, leaping from his saddle into a battle-ready stance. He gripped a huge two-handed sword in his fists.

The shaddim drifted nearer, steadily tightening a circle around us. The closer they got, the louder and more frenzied their moaning became.

Uncle Arick didn't stand a chance.

The shaddim were ghosts darker than anything I'd ever seen. Shaped like tall, narrow triangles, they reminded me of wisps of smoke with curling, snake tails where their legs and feet should be. They had long arms that looked stretched-out and scissor blade claws the length of my forearm.

Their shining yellow eyes stared at me. When their mouths opened to moan, whatever was behind them showed through like I was looking out a window. The monsters were hollow and razor-thin.

Ooowhooo-ooh-ooo.

The noise deafened me. It echoed in my mind and whispered greedily. *Give us the Horn*, it seemed to say. *Mother wants the Horn*.

"Jasiah, look out!" Kadze cried.

A dark, thin arm snapped at me like a tentacle. Razored claws whisked inches from my face.

Then Kadze was there, leaping between me and the shaddim. He was fast, very fast. His arms and legs sliced through the air in a blur like a knight's deadly weapons.

I twisted away, pulling hard on Chet's reins. In a stuttering lurch, we nearly bowled Uncle Arick over.

He held a cluster of shaddim at bay with his mighty sword, slashing its point threateningly at the monsters as they tried to advance.

From the corner of his eye, he spotted me. "Don't let them touch you!" he warned without looking from the shaddim. "One touch will put you to sleep."

Chet fidgeted nervously. He was well-trained and brave, but the constant moaning was still scaring him. He would run soon, and I wouldn't be able to stop him.

"What do I do?" I wailed helplessly.

A shaddim struck at Uncle Arick before my uncle could respond. His sword took the creature at the elbow, passing through the arm as if it were fog.

Unharmed, the monster moaned louder and lashed out

16

with its arm again.

"Run, Jasiah!" my uncle ordered. "Run to Tiller's Field and find Wizard Ast."

I blinked in shock. I wasn't a hero, but I still knew right from wrong. "I can't! I can't leave—" I tried to protest.

Bending suddenly at the knees and pivoting to his right, Uncle Arick parried another shaddim attack. Then with one hand, he pulled something bulky from a sack on his belt.

"Take this and go," he commanded. "This quest is about you. Go, now!"

He tossed the object to me, and I clumsily caught it while struggling to maintain my grip on the reins. The object was an oversized, right-handed gauntlet made of heavy leather.

I wanted to ask what I was supposed to do with it but didn't have the time. Uncle Arick swatted Chet on the rump and sent us charging though the ranks of the shaddim.

Whip-like arms and claws swatted at us. Empty mouths split wide and moaned. It was like galloping blind through a tangled forest. I squeezed my eyes shut and held my breath.

Ooowhooo-ooh-ooo.

Not until the moaning died did I open my eyes and risk a glance backward.

Uncle Arick stood in the center of the road, completely surrounded. His enormous sword flashed again and again.

Behind him lay Kadze. The boy's chest rose and fell with the breathing of sleep, but other than that, he didn't move.

17

When I saw my uncle trip and go down, I buried my face in Chet's mane and shrieked without a sound. There was nothing else I could do.

We charged into the night, hunted and alone.

3

What have I done? What have I done? I asked myself guiltily with every step westward. Cool autumn wind buffeted my face but my cheeks burned warmly with shame.

I'd left my uncle and friend in danger.

They had stayed behind to fight while ordering me to run. They'd sacrificed themselves so that I could escape. *Why?*

The mysterious answer came to me right away. *This quest is about you*, Uncle Arick had said. How I wished I knew what that meant!

I pulled up rein and turned back to peer down Wagonwheel Road. Uncle Arick and Kadze were some-where in the deepening gloom, probably fighting for their lives. Maybe Kadze was still unconscious. Maybe Uncle Arick was, too.

I wanted to race to save them, and I wanted to hide in a

place where I could never be found. Not by shaddim. Not by wizards and their quests. But I couldn't make myself move. I was frozen with fear and indecision.

Uncle Arick's words repeated in my head, and I tried desperately to understand them.

How is the quest about me? Because I have the same name as the Horn? If that were true, the quest should be about Uncle Arick, too. His name was also Dragonsbane.

Nothing made sense, and I shook my head as chaotic images flashed through my mind. The appearance of the shaddim. Kadze charging to my rescue. Uncle Arick telling me to run and giving me—

The gauntlet! It was still in my hand.

I stared at it thoughtfully for only a moment. There was no way I'd let a second mystery add to my confusion.

I slid my hand inside and strapped it on.

The gauntlet was dark brown and covered with lighter streaks like scratch marks. It was also much too big for me and hung limply from my arm like the baggy clothing on a scarecrow. It reached all the way to my shoulder.

I studied the scratches on its surface, imagining they were cuts from a sword blade. Then I shook my arm in annoyance.

"Another mystery…" I started to mutter when the gauntlet came to life.

Skrrrinch! It tightened over my skin, warming alarmingly. I cried out and tore at the straps and buckles that fastened it, but they would budge. My right arm, hand, and fingers were being mummified!

"What's happening?" I gasped aloud. Beneath me, Chet shifted nervously.

Suddenly, the gauntlet's transformation ended. It cooled and the pressure on my arm decreased.

When I glanced down, the gauntlet was perfectly sized to fit my hand and arm. It felt snug but not tight, and covered my forearm like a stretched sock.

The gauntlet was magic without a doubt. But knowing that didn't tell my anything helpful. It was more of a mystery than when I'd put it on.

Thwitch!

The sound of a snapping stick echoed sharply nearby. Muffled voices drifted in from the darkness.

Someone was coming!

At first I hoped the voices belonged to Uncle Arick and Kadze, but the sounds had come from behind me, and I'd turned around. Kadze and my uncle were ahead of me.

I forgot all about the gauntlet and frantically scanned the shadows for somewhere to hide.

Strangers on an empty road at night would certainly be up to no good.

4

"Who's there?" called a girl's voice.

"We can see you," a boy's added, "so don't try anything funny. I'm deputy of Tiller's Field."

A boy deputy? I'll bet, I thought doubtfully. Besides, if they could really see me, they should've been able to tell that I was a small boy without weapons.

I searched the darkness but couldn't make out anything except the trail of Wagonwheel Road and the dark shapes of leafless trees.

That was odd. My special vision wasn't usually fooled by darkness. I should have spotted the strangers.

I clutched Chet's reins tighter, preparing to flee when the girl's clear voice suddenly rang out.

Stars and moon, I summon thee.
Bright as noon this pebble be.

When her chant ended, a tiny light winked ahead of me. It flared and then arced forward like it had been tossed underhand, glowing ever brighter.

Plip! It landed near Chet's hooves and exploded in a blinding white brilliance.

Chet whinnied in alarm and reared back, nearly tossing me to the ground. "*W*-whoa!" I cried awkwardly. "Whoa!" I didn't know much about calming a spooked horse.

The light shone from a small, flat stone in the middle of the road. Its radiance completely surrounded me and Chet. We were caught, totally visible in the night.

Since I didn't know what else to do, I took a chance. "Wizard Ast?" I asked, squinting to see beyond the light.

I knew the wizard wasn't a young girl or boy, but I hoped using his name would convince the pair of strangers that I was Wizard Ast's friend.

To my relief, it worked.

"Jasiah?" came the girl's reply. She sounded frightened and hopeful at the same time.

I blinked in surprise. Aside from Wizard Ast, I hadn't expected anyone from Tiller's Field to know my name. I was a long way from home.

"Yes, I'm Jasiah," I said in my lowest voice. I tried to sound confident and brave but ended up stuttering. "*W*-who is it?"

After a short pause, a boy and girl stepped into the light, appearing almost as suddenly as shaddim. The boy was

23

around my age, maybe a year or two older, and had thick, dark hair. The girl was tall, blonde, and wore a skirt decorated with horses.

"We're so glad to see you!" she exclaimed. "I'm Jozlyn and this is my baby brother Josh. Wizard Ast sent us to find you."

Josh shot his sister a dirty look but didn't say anything. I guess he didn't appreciate being called *baby*. Babies weren't given fancy deputy's badges like the one pinned to his left breast.

"Why, is something wrong?" I asked. "Where's the wizard?"

This time, Josh replied. "We'll tell you all about it, but we have to hide first. There's some strange, moaning creatures nearby."

I gasped and my eyes went wide. Josh was talking about shaddim. That meant he'd seen them and that they were hunting from every direction. Tiller's Field wasn't safe and neither was the way I'd come.

"Let's hurry," I said urgently. Josh and Jozlyn might not know much about the shaddim, but I did. We needed to hide. Fast.

Jozlyn nodded and pointed off the road to her right. "This way," she said. "We'll be safe in Dreamsafe Den. It's not far."

As we started off the road, I couldn't help thinking guiltily of Uncle Arick and Kadze again. Had they found a place to hide, too?

More importantly, was Jozlyn's secret place safe from ghosts like shaddim?

Say it, Not Eat it

5

During the five or ten minutes it took to reach Dreamsafe Den, I imagined all sorts of destinations. A cave hidden behind a boulder. A huge hollow tree. A farmer's cozy barn full of mooing cows.

We made the trip in silence. No one mentioned it, but we were afraid to make unnecessary noise. In the darkness, our breathing sounded as loud as the heaving bellows in a blacksmith's forge.

We certainly didn't talk about shaddim. They were close. They were hunting. That was plenty to keep us moving fast and quietly.

At last Jozlyn held up a hand to signal a stop. I looked about eagerly for something unusual, but nothing looked out of the ordinary.

We stood in a small clearing. A fallen tree with grey bark was perched at a sloping angle in the center. Tall, multicolored flowers surrounded it in a thick patch. They stood almost as high as our knees.

"Here we are," Jozlyn whispered. "Dreamsafe Den." Next to her, Josh grinned.

I glanced at them, then at the tree and flowers. There was no room for people to hide, let alone Chet. "Here we are *where*?"

Jozlyn bent to pick one of the flowers. "Take this," she said, offering it to me. It had alternating pink and blue petals shaped like tiny pillows. "You'll see in a second."

I accepted the flower as she and Josh picked ones for themselves. Jozlyn actually plucked two. The flowers gave off a warm scent of vanilla.

"Now, repeat after me," Jozlyn instructed. Josh continued to grin like he had a big secret to share, and I got the feeling I was in for a surprise.

Jozlyn cleared her throat then chanted the silly verses to a spell.

A sapling's seed,
A buzzing bee,
A falling flake,
A plattered pea—

Oh how I hope
To shrink my size
So may we meet
With eyes to eyes.

When she finished, Jozlyn looked at me expectantly. "Go ahead," she encouraged.

I swallowed slowly before beginning. "A sapling's seed…a buzzing bee…uh…a yucky pea?" I finally gave up, totally lost. "*Bleh!* I hate peas. Can we change that part?"

Josh chuckled but Jozlyn rolled her eyes at me. "You have to *say* it, not *eat* it," she grumped. "What's wrong with boys?"

That question, I knew, wasn't supposed to be answered.

"I'm sorry. I'm trying," I apologized. I hadn't known Jozlyn for more than fifteen minutes and she already felt like *my* big sister.

"All right, we'll say it together," she compromised. "Josh, you say it, too."

We made it through the words of the spell on the third try. Jozlyn said each line first. Josh and I repeated them.

I whispered the last line with my eyes squeezed shut, expecting something magical to happen. It didn't. No fireworks exploded. No secret hideaway mysteriously appeared.

"How long do we have to wait?" I asked while frowning at my flower. *Why am I holding this stupid thing anyway? I should have known a teenaged girl can't do magic.*

This time it was Jozlyn's turn to smirk. "Smell your flower," she shrugged.

I looked at her suspiciously and then at Josh. He nodded, so I held the flower to my nose and inhaled.

28

The overpowering scent of vanilla made me sneeze. Once, twice, and then three times. When I opened my eyes, the world looked frighteningly—

Big.

Trees with smooth green skin surrounded me, and a strange, tube-shaped wooden building rose up like a mountain directly ahead. Even the sky looked different, somehow impossibly far away.

"What…?" I gasped in astonishment. *Is it me, or do those trees look like giant flowers?*

Before I finished the thought, I realized what had happened. The trees *were* flowers. Just like the one in my hand but bigger. Actually, they were normal-sized and I was small.

Jozlyn's magic had worked. I was three inches tall!

An enormous shadow fell over me, and a deep voice rumbled from far above.

"OOOOHHH!" it bellowed, rattling my teeth.

Without thinking, I started to run. The shaddim had found me again!

Dreamsafe Den

6

THUMPH! An enormous black boot crashed down in front of me before I took three steps.

"JASIAH, HOLD STILL!" boomed Josh's voice so loudly I almost lost my balance. "WE'RE COMING!"

Jozlyn's deafening giggle vibrated in my chest as a thick scent of vanilla filled the air again. The powerful smell made me cringe. Who knew what else the magical flowers could do?

Sneezing, Jozlyn, Josh, and Chet appeared, no longer looking like giants. The two kids smiled at me and chuckled like they'd just shared a good joke.

At my expense, I sulked.

"Why'd you scare me like that," I demanded, "with all the moaning?"

Jozlyn blinked. "Moaning—*oh!*" She laughed and

30

nudged Josh in the ribs. "I didn't moan. I'd wanted to say, *Oooohhh, look at the little pixie boy*, but you started running."

I frowned, more to myself than at her. It wasn't Jozlyn's fault that I had an overactive imagination.

"Here, look!" She pulled a pink pixie doll from a satchel over her shoulder. "This is Rosie. She's a pixie and the one who told me about this place. For a little bit, you looked just her size."

I groaned. *A doll? Aren't you too old to play with dolls?* But aloud, I said, "Sure, she's great."

Josh must've noticed the sour look on my face. "Trust me," he whispered so his sister couldn't hear, "it's better to go along with her." In a louder voice, he added, "Let's get inside before we really do hear something moaning."

Thankfully, the talk of Rosie the pixie doll ended there. Josh led us through the flower forest and into one end of the fallen log. We left Chet outside in a miniature corral made of stacked dandelion stems like a log cabin. Two other horses already grazed in the corral.

To my amazement, the log's interior wasn't rotting, smelly, damp, or filled with bugs. It was actually one of the most comfortable, relaxing places I'd ever been.

Toadstool tables and chairs formed an elegant dining area in one end. Hollowed acorn shells filled with berries, nuts, and morning dew made delicious centerpieces.

Farther inside, a cozy fire burned cheerfully, its smoke

31

disappearing through a rounded knot in the ceiling. Moss and leaf-twined nests circled the hearth at a safe distance.

The whole place glowed warmly from winking fireflies that hovered near the ceiling.

"It's wonderful," I murmured in surprise. I'd never imagined such a place. *How many secrets like this*, I wondered, *do I miss every day by not paying closer attention to things?*

"I told you Dreamsafe Den was the place to hide," Jozlyn said. She grabbed Josh and me by our elbows and yanked us toward a table. "Let's eat!"

We didn't have to be asked twice. Running from shaddim and shrinking down to pixie size was hungry business.

After dinner, we quickly agreed that it was too late to leave. Morning would be a better time, not to mention the shaddim didn't hunt in the daylight.

"But we can't go to Tiller's Field," Jozlyn announced. "Those creatures—the *shaddim*—attacked. Everyone's asleep or hiding, even Wizard Ast."

"What?" I exclaimed. "I've got to see him. He summoned me for a quest."

Josh held up his hands to try to calm me. "We know," he explained. "Wizard Ast summoned us, too. We're all part of the quest."

I shook my head in frustration. I didn't know the first thing about quests or the Dragonsbane Horn. How was I supposed to know what to do without Wizard Ast?

"The wizard gave us some instructions," Jozlyn added. "Before he went off to fight the shaddim, he told us to find you and…and to give you this."

She took a large, leather book from her satchel and placed it gently on the table. It was obviously old and had a square, silver lock on its front cover. Scratch marks gouged the lock like someone had tried to pick or pry it open.

"We didn't do that," Josh said when he saw me staring at the scratches. "It was like that when we got it. Wizard Ast told us that only you could open it."

That surprised me. Why would I be able to unlock the book? I didn't have a key.

Uncle Arick's mysterious words echoed in my mind again. *This quest is about you.* Maybe he'd meant the book. Maybe he thought I could unlock it.

"So…" Jozlyn urged with an eager smile tugging her lips, "…open it."

I stared at the thick book for a long time before reaching across the table. Except for the lock, it was fairly plain and looked like a girl's oversized diary.

When my fingers brushed its cover, the book suddenly growled and lurched into the air, glowing with a faint golden light. I snatched at it timidly, but it was too high above me.

Josh's toadstool chair flew back with a squishy *sploot*, and he was on his feet. In his hand was a slim sword that flickered with blue flames along its blade.

I took my eyes from the book long enough to gawk at him. Uncle Arick's gauntlet, Jozlyn's flowers, the book, Josh's sword. Was I the only person who thought magic was unusual?

"Watch out!" Josh cried, looking every bit the deputy of Tiller's Field. He threw a protective arm in front of Jozlyn while I took a step back.

We watched the book cautiously as it floated just out of reach. It rotated several times, then *click*, its lock popped open. Slowly it drifted back to the table as gracefully as a feather.

It landed front-side up facing me.

We stared at it in silence before Jozlyn finally spoke. "Well, isn't one of you brave boys going to open it?"

My eyes darted from her to the book. Somehow I'd unlocked it, so I figured opening it was my job, too.

I reached for the book with one shaky hand.

7

As my fingers inched closer to the book, it suddenly jumped at me like a snarling dog trying to bite my hand. I cried out but caught it with my right hand, the one protected by Uncle Arick's gauntlet.

Even through the thick leather, the book felt warm and alive. It pulsed with the rhythm of a beating heart.

Throomp-throomp, the steady beat drummed into my fingertips. *THROOMP-throomp*, it vibrated up into my hand.

Josh and Jozlyn watched me without breathing. *Open it*, Jozlyn mouthed silently.

I hoped there were answers inside the book. Answers about the Dragonsbane Horn and our quest. Maybe even answers about me and about why Uncle Arick thought I was so important.

I took a deep breath and swallowed hard. Opening a

book shouldn't have been so frightening, but it was. I was afraid that I might not like what I saw inside.

My delay seemed to irritate the book.

THROOMP-THROOMP! It thumped harder than ever, so hard that I had to cradle it against my chest to keep it steady. With my free hand, I clawed the cover open.

THROO—

The beating stopped.

Golden light seeped from the book like a leak in a hose. Fascinated, I stared at it, unable to pull my eyes away. It slowly took on a recognizable shape like a lump of clay spinning on a wheel.

A brilliant golden dragon appeared. As transparent as a ghost, the dragon floated above the table and rotated slowly. Its snakelike lower half wound a smoky trail down into the book.

When the dragon's piercing, orange eyes met mine, my skin tingled as if I were standing too close to a fire. Sweat dampened my clothes, and my thoughts vanished like dry pine needles put to a torch.

I couldn't look away. I couldn't remember my name. All I knew was the dragon and its words. Nothing else mattered.

In a deep, airy voice that sounded like the surf roaring during a storm, it spoke. *"Listen well, Jasiah, and remember. This quest is about you. Others will follow but only you shall lead."*

Images and faces of people filled my mind. On a mountaintop, a man stood before a crowd with the Dragonsbane Horn held above his head. He spoke strange words I couldn't understand then threw the Horn over the side of a cliff.

Even hypnotized by the dragon's vision, I knew that I was seeing the past. The dragon was showing me the history of the Horn.

Next, I saw the Horn floating. It hovered in the air like a circling bird, then exploded. Four flames blazed from the blast, streaking the sky like shooting stars. They raced through the air in different directions and disappeared.

I watched them go and the vision faded. Sweat matted my hair to my face, and I was shivering, but not from cold.

The dragon fell silent and watched me with its glowing eyes. It wanted me to understand what I'd seen. It wanted me to know what had to be done.

The quest—*our* quest—was to go on the world's most important scavenger hunt. The Horn had been magically split into four parts and scattered throughout the land. We needed to find them and put them together.

I looked into the dragon's eyes. Somehow I knew it could read my thoughts. *I know what to do*, I told it without words. *But where do we begin our search for the four pieces?*

The dragon tilted its head toward the book. *Read, Jasiah*, it whispered in my mind.

I waited, expecting it to tell me more. I still had so many questions. *Why was the quest about me? Why did the shaddim hunt me?*

The dragon finally opened its mouth to speak, but flinched as if waking from a nightmare instead. Its golden light flickered and dulled like it had drifted beneath a shadow or—

Like a shadow had slithered into it.

The dragon blinked slowly, a mischievous grin splitting its lips. When its eyes opened, they blazed red with hate.

"Come to me, Dragonsbane," the dragon hissed as dry as a snake's scales. "Bring the book to Shelolth before my shaddim take it from you by force."

I gasped and fell back, tripping over my toadstool chair. From the floor, I cried out. "*What*—who are you?"

Something *had* slipped into the golden dragon. Something dark and terribly evil.

The new dragon chuckled. "I am Shelolth. You must bring the book to me—*now!*"

The dragon's mouth gaped, displaying rows and rows of barbed fangs. A blackened tongue snaked out to lick black lips.

"*NOW!*" she howled as black flames spewed from her mouth.

I threw up my arms but knew it was hopeless. I was about to be burned to a crisp.

8

In a roaring funnel, Shelolth the dragon's fiery breath erupted straight at me. Dark flames whipped and flailed like the arms of shrieking ghosts.

I shrieked, too, and flattened myself against the floor. The flames were coming closer, hissing, burning....

"Close the book!" Josh cried. I couldn't see him through the blaze, but I heard him loud and clear.

I slammed Wizard Ast's book shut like it was the snapping jaw of a dragon. Heat washed over me and then—

Nothing.

I pried my eyes open, surprised to find them squeezed shut. But surprised, mostly, to find myself alive.

Shelolth and her fire were gone. Not a single burn mark or ash remained. We were safe.

"*What*—who was that?" Jozlyn stammered. She knelt beside me with a worried look on her face.

"Her name is Shelolth," I replied slowly. "She's a dragon. I think the shaddim are her servants."

Saying the words made me shudder. The shaddim were plenty dangerous by themselves. Knowing Shelolth was powerful enough to boss them around terrified me.

"So now what?" I asked to change the subject. I didn't want to talk about Shelolth or shaddim.

Josh crouched down and tapped the book on my lap. "We have to read it," he said firmly.

I gawked at him but Jozlyn nodded. "The golden dragon told us to," she agreed.

Told me *to*, I corrected silently. *The quest is about me. The reading is up to me. Me, me, me!*

Being a hero on a quest is big trouble, I decided, especially when dragons and magic books are involved.

"Fine," I snapped, "but if fire shoots out and up my nose when I open it, I'm blaming you two."

Jozlyn giggled and Josh rolled his eyes. "Just read it," he prodded. "Shelolth is gone."

Expecting the worst, I flipped open the book's cover. I cringed as I did it but nothing happened—no light, no fire, no dragon. The book was as stationary as a rock.

Surprisingly, the thick book had only one page. Words written in a flowing, golden script formed the words to a poem, so I read them aloud.

One waits with the wizard
In his hollow tome.
One sounds in the sands
Of the dwarven home.
One rings wrapped in roots
In damp forest loam.
One drones in the dark
Where the shaddim roam.

Four for the future.
Four 'fore the reign.
Four for the forging
Of Horn Dragonsbane.

The words vanished after I read them, and then the whole page disappeared. Where it had been was an opening like the inside of a box.

That's why it's so thick, I realized. *It's hollow.* Something metal and tube-shaped rested snugly inside the book-box.

"The Horn!" Jozlyn gasped.

Sure enough, the object was slightly curved and shaped like the horn on a bull's head. One end was jagged and sharp as if it had been snapped off from a larger piece. The other end narrowed to a round opening.

"No…" I said, thinking out loud, "…a piece of the Horn…."

Suddenly I understood the first line of the poem. The *hollow tome* was the book-box in my hands, and the *wizard* was Wizard Ast.

We'd already found the first piece of the Horn!

"I get it!" Josh exclaimed. "The poem gave us clues about where to find the pieces of the Horn."

Jozlyn's face brightened. "You're right. That means the second part of the poem should tell us where to find the next piece."

She looked at me eagerly. "Tell us the second part again."

To my surprise, I remembered it. In fact, I remembered the whole poem like I'd spent hours memorizing it.

I cleared my throat then recited the lines.

One sounds in the sands
Of the dwarven home.

Silence followed as we tried to puzzle out the meaning to the words. It seemed obvious and easy, but we were afraid to say it out loud.

Silvermight.

As the old stories went, Silvermight had been a shining city in the Glittersgold Mountains where the dwarven people lived. But the city had supposedly been devoured by a hungry sea of sand. No one had seen it in centuries.

The three of us knew the stories, but we also knew the difference between fact and fiction. Sand didn't eat cities! Silvermight had never really existed.

Still, the clues in the poem hinted at Silvermight. The answer could only be one place.

"Silvermight," Jozlyn finally whispered.

Josh snorted and gave her a funny look. "Silvermight doesn't exist. It's just a legend."

Jozlyn ignored him and looked at me. "Let Jasiah decide," she said. "He's the leader."

I wanted to protest, but I knew she was right. The golden dragon had said so. *Many will follow but only you will lead*, were its exact words.

That meant I was in charge of the quest for the Dragonsbane Horn. Making decisions was my responsibility.

I swallowed hard, thinking of all the wondrous magic I'd seen recently—gauntlets, shaddim, dragons, shrinking spells, and more. Was a city eaten by sand so hard to imagine?

I shook my head. No, it wasn't. After all the magic I'd seen, I could believe in ghost stories, too.

"Silvermight," I murmured, my voice cracking. "That's where we'll find the next piece of the Horn."

Sticks Aren't for Kids

9

I barely slept that night. Dreams of the shaddim and Shelolth kept me tossing and turning. I even dreamed that the Horn had been swallowed by a dragon.

When Josh nudged me awake, my eyes felt like they were full of sand. "It's time to go," he said.

I blinked at him tiredly. Did facing danger ever wear him out? Had he always been a courageous deputy? He and Jozlyn both seemed so much braver than me, always ready for action.

We ate a small breakfast of berries and milk then went outside. The sky was dark and full of swirling, black clouds. If we hadn't just awakened, I'd have thought it was evening. The day was that dreary.

Jozlyn led us to the dandelion corral where Chet and the other two horses had spent the night. She whispered to the three of them then opened the gate. The horses charged out and stopped a short distance away to graze.

"Time to grow," she said, turning to me and Josh with a smile. Then she took our flowers from her satchel.

I blinked again, this time in surprise. I'd forgotten about our being small. I guess it's easy to get used to new things if you give them a try—even to shrinking!

We held the flowers to our noses and inhaled their sweet vanilla scent. In seconds, the three of us and the horses were normal-sized and ready to go.

Josh's horse was solid white except for a black patch on his nose. His name was Honormark and Josh had borrowed him from a friend.

Jozlyn climbed aboard her black horse with white socks. I figured the horse's name would be something like *Boots*, but Jozlyn surprised me.

"This is Broomstick," she said, stroking the horse's head gently.

"*Broomstick?* Don't witches ride brooms?" I joked, nudging Josh with my elbow.

Jozlyn glared at me. The look was the same older sister stare she used on Josh. It worked on me, too. I felt my face flush and dropped my eyes to my feet.

"I prefer to think of myself as an enchantress," she said seriously.

My eyes shot back up to hers. "You mean you're really a witch?" I couldn't believe it. She was too young to be a witch—an enchantress, whatever.

46

Jozlyn narrowed her eyes. The new look was anything but sisterly. "You believe my brother can be a deputy but that I can't be an enchantress?"

Oops! I'd really put my foot in it. My mouth, that is.

"*N*-no," I stammered. "That's not what I'm saying." But wasn't that *exactly* what I'd said?

"Uh-huh," Jozlyn replied, folding her arms over her chest. Josh started to snicker but Jozlyn shot him a dirty look.

I threw up my arms. Of course I knew a girl could be an enchantress. She could be a deputy, too, for all I cared. A girl could be anything a boy could be.

"Witches ride broomsticks," I argued weakly.

"Shows what you know," Jozlyn sassed. "Broomstick is as close to riding a real broom as I'll get. Ugly, old witches ride brooms. Kids don't. Besides, think of the splinters!"

When she smiled, so did I, and our disagreement was over. She was an enchantress. Josh was a deputy. And I was a dope with a big mouth.

The idea of kids flying around on brooms like witches did make me laugh though.

I quickly climbed onto Chet, and we said goodbye to Dreamsafe Den. I hated to leave the place because I doubted we'd enjoy safe, comfortable beds again for weeks.

We trotted along Wagonwheel Road a short distance then turned north. Josh advised against passing through Tiller's Field, and Jozlyn and I agreed. Shaddim might still be lurking about the village.

The lost city of Silvermight had been located in the middle of the Glittersgold Mountains, now a desert ocean called the Sandy Sea. That was at least a week's ride west of Everleaf Woods. We couldn't afford running into trouble.

Unfortunately, trouble ran into us.

After a brief stop for lunch, we turned west again. Tiller's Field was safely south and to our left. Gurgleburp Creek was just ahead.

"We'll have to wade across the water," Josh said. "The only bridge is near town."

Right away, I didn't like the idea of getting wet. The weather hadn't improved, and the temperature had dropped. Our breath and the breath of our horses were white puffs in the chilly air.

"Can't we go around?" I asked.

Josh cocked his head at me. "Around a river?"

"Umm…" I muttered, knowing I didn't have a good response. Sometimes I just didn't think before speaking.

Ooowhooo-ooh-ooo.

The familiar, chilling moan of the shaddim interrupted before I could say more.

I wheeled Chet about to see a pack of grisly shaddim floating down the rise of a steep hill. Their dark, ghostly bodies fluttered like blankets hanging from a clothesline.

What are they doing here? I wondered in a panic. *It isn't night!*

"Run!" Jozlyn shrieked, crouching low in her saddle. Her long hair streamed behind her like a banner.

Ooowhooo-ooh-ooo.

Gurgleburp Creek came into view almost immediately. Gurgling, burping water cut a wide path through the grassy field.

At first I thought we were saved. All we had to do was get to the other side. We could keep the creek between us and the shaddim.

But there was one problem. We had no way to get ourselves across. We were trapped and running into a dead end.

Ooowhooo-ooh-ooo.

Hop 'n Fly Horse

10

Jozlyn raced toward Gurgleburp Creek like a knight charging across a battlefield. Josh galloped close behind.

Coming in fast, the shaddim gave chase. Their razor-thin arms slashed the air like whips.

Ooowhooo-ooh-ooo.

"Move!" Josh roared, and I gave a start.

I'd been standing still watching! The shaddim were almost on top of me.

Snarling wildly, I urged Chet to run. The shaddim reached for me, their claws slicing. Shivers crawled over my skin.

One touch and they'd have me.

Suddenly, Josh appeared with his flaming blue sword in hand. He chopped and slashed at the shaddim, forcing them back.

"Go, go!" he cried. "Hurry!"

With a final thrust, Josh spun around and we charged after Jozlyn. We caught her halfway to the creek.

"We're going to jump," she shouted, bringing Broomstick along side us at a gallop. "On three!"

"Just count fast," Josh told her.

Instead of responding, Jozlyn gracefully raised her arms above her head. Broomstick never slowed, and I don't know how Jozlyn didn't fall. She was a superb rider!

Clutching her tiny broom, she chanted a ridiculous rhyme.

Frogs can hop and birds can fly.
What's to stop a horse's try?

Count to three and hold on tight.
We'll soar free in equine flight!

She snatched Broomstick's reins when she'd finished and crouched in the saddle again. "Remember, on three!"

That's it? I cried silently. *A silly rhyme?* We weren't shrinking to fit into a fairy hideout. We were running for our lives. Shouldn't important magic be more serious?

"One!" Jozlyn shouted.

I glanced over my shoulder to see the shaddim right behind us. Their outstretched arms clawed at the tails of our horses. Their burning eyes promised terror.

"Two!" she continued.

I forced myself to concentrate on the creek. The water

51

was coming in fast.

"Three!"

Jozlyn hauled back on her reins. Josh did the same. First Broomstick and then Honormark leaped into the air.

It was time to jump, only I'd forgotten one important detail. I didn't know how to make a horse jump.

11

Stale air like the breath of a corpse slashed against my cheek. Its stench made my eyes water, and tears streamed down my face.

I didn't need to look to know what was happening. The shaddim were on top of me, slashing and moaning. Trying to put me to sleep.

Bouncing dizzily, I was almost to the near bank of Gurgleburp Creek. I had to jump—

Now!

I leaned back, pulled up, and closed my eyes. Chet did the rest. One second we were pounding across the ground, the next we were floating.

I took a huge, refreshing breath and opened my eyes as we started to drop. For some reason, I felt no fear.

Chet's landing was incredibly soft, and Jozlyn smiled proudly at me. "Still don't believe I'm an enchantress?"

she teased.

I smiled breathlessly but couldn't speak. I was too stunned. The three of us had just jumped twenty-five feet over moving water.

No horse and rider could do that!

But we had, and we'd escaped the shaddim. They moaned angrily from the far side of the creek then floated south toward Tiller's Field.

We all let out sighs of relief. Our gamble had worked. The shaddim couldn't cross water.

"They're heading for Mosswood Bridge," Josh said. "That gives us a good head start. Let's use it." He clicked his tongue, coaxing Honormark into a trot. Jozlyn and I followed in silence.

As we left Gurgleburp Creek behind, a dark mass of trees appeared on our left. Even though it was autumn, the trees still held their leaves. It was a disturbing sight. The leaves were black and covered with green splotches like moldy bread.

"The leaves never fall," Jozlyn explained when she noticed me staring at the gloomy trees. "That's why the forest is called Everleaf Woods."

I quickly turned away from the trees. Moldy, black leaves weren't natural. They should've turned brown and fallen from the branches.

"Most trees and forests go to sleep in the winter," Jozlyn continued, "but not Everleaf Woods."

Josh pulled up next to us. "Everleaf Woods gets angry," he added.

My eyes followed his to the trees, and I shuddered. The blackness of the woods reminded me of shaddim. "We don't have to go in there, do we?"

Josh shared a curious look with his sister then shook his head. "No," he answered, "we're going around. The woods aren't safe."

From there we rode in silence for several hours. The depressing wall of trees stretched on endlessly, and none of us felt much like talking.

I was starting to think we'd never reach the end of the trees when a faint sound reached my ears.

Crrr-eeeeak.

"Did you hear that?" I hissed, cupping a hand around my ear and drawing Chet to a stop.

"Hear what?" Jozlyn asked.

I concentrated, waiting for the sound again. I realized that Josh and Jozlyn couldn't hear as well as I could.

I didn't wait long.

Crrr-eeeeak.

"There," I said. "Something's coming. Sounds like a wagon."

Josh quickly tugged his reins, turning Honormark toward the trees. "We have to hide."

I glanced from him to the forest and then back to him. "In there?" I gulped.

He nodded without taking his eyes from Everleaf Woods. "Three kids alone—we'd have to answer too many questions."

Numbly, I nodded. We didn't have a choice. Whoever was coming might be too interested in what we were doing. We had to protect our piece of the Horn and finish our quest.

"Let's go," Josh hissed, "but stay close to one another."

Like grave robbers sneaking into a tomb, we quietly slinked into the deadly black of Everleaf Woods.

12

I'd never been so afraid. Not of shaddim. Not of Shelolth. As we ducked behind the nightmarish trees of Everleaf Woods, I feared I'd never see the sun again.

Josh held a finger to his lips and pointed through the tangle of trees. The wagon was coming.

Crrr-eeeeak.

It approached slowly, wheels creaking like old bones. When it stopped on the road in front of our hiding place, I gasped at the sight of it.

The wagon was difficult to look at. Painted in dazzling yellow and pale green stripes, it actually stung my eyes. Bright pink and purple lettering spelled out the words

Medium Mirelda's Volacious Vardo

on its side.

A vardo is a kind of wagon used by traveling gypsies. Inside I imagined crystal balls, fortune-telling cards, and dangling strings of beads and shiny trinkets. The outside shimmered like waves of heat rising from a steamy street.

From inside, a woman's voice called out in a thick accent. "It is time for meeting," she said, and I had to concentrate to make out her words. "You make coming out now."

I squinted at Jozlyn and Josh. *Make coming out?* I repeated silently, mouthing the words.

Josh shushed me with an annoyed wave. "Be quiet," he ordered between clenched teeth.

Oh sure, I thought. He was the one speaking out loud. I opened my mouth to respond.

"Hush, you knuckleheads," Jozlyn hissed, eyeing us in her older sister way. The look dared us to speak.

We snapped our mouths shut and turned back to the wagon. It hadn't moved, but something I'd missed earlier sent an icy tingle up my spine. There was nothing pulling the wagon, or pushing either!

It moved by magic.

A peach-painted trapdoor on its roof suddenly flipped open and a small white object whizzed out. It zigzagged through the air, buzzing like a swarm of mosquitoes.

I went perfectly still as the object zipped this way and that like a curious dog investigating new scents. In almost no time, it made its way into the trees.

"We have to run," I whispered without moving my lips. We were only a few hours from Tiller's Field. Our quest had just begun. We couldn't stand around waiting to be caught.

Josh turned to me and nodded slowly, then we both looked at Jozlyn. Her eyes were wide and her face pale. With one shaky finger, she pointed over my shoulder.

The whining buzz vibrated in my ears, and I turned my head slowly, afraid of what I'd see. It was the flying white object. Only it wasn't completely white or just any old object.

It was an eyeball, a gooey, floating eyeball.

It stared at me and blinked slowly like a raven with its head cocked. "I am seeing you," said the mysterious voice from the wagon.

13

"Yah!" shouted Jozlyn, urging Broomstick to flee.

"Yah!" Josh echoed fiercely.

"*Aah!*" I screamed when the eyeball blinked again.

How it blinked without an eyelid, I'll never know. But I swear it did.

We charged out of Everleaf Woods, branches and black leaves clawing at us like the stiff arms of zombies. The gaudy wagon was straight ahead, and Jozlyn shot to its right. Josh and I followed without question.

Immediately a bad feeling knotted my stomach. I knew we shouldn't go right—not back toward Tiller's Field—but it was too late to say anything.

We had a flying, buzzing, blinking eyeball chasing us! That was plenty to worry about.

Ahead of me, Broomstick's galloping hooves were a blur. They pounded the ground and threw up clods of dirt.

Behind me, the buzzing eyeball droned in pursuit.

The horses couldn't run forever. They would tire and need rest. Could they outlast the eyeball?

Jozlyn led our escape, and I bounced behind, praying not to fall. I was a terrible rider and wished Kadze were in the saddle with me again. He'd have easily kept us in a straight line.

Even with the gypsy wagon and the eyeball on my heels, I realized that I missed Kadze and Uncle Arick. *Had they escaped the shaddim?* I worried. *Would I ever see them again?*

"Hold up!" Josh called, interrupting my thoughts. I wasn't sure how long or far we'd galloped, but I was glad for the break.

Immediately, I noticed something different. The air was silent and still, and the buzzing of the eyeball was gone.

"Did we outrun them?" I panted. Somehow, riding a horse wore me out.

Josh spun Honormark in a circle, carefully searching for danger. To our right, Everleaf Woods blotted out the sky. A small cluster of leafless trees marked the edge of the forest. Every other direction was clear.

"I think we're safe," Jozlyn exhaled. She said it as her eyes darted back and forth nervously.

I sure didn't feel safe. We might have escaped the eyeball but we weren't out of danger. Nowhere was truly safe, not while we were on the quest for the Dragonsbane

Horn.

A shadowy flicker caught my eye. Something dark had moved in the cluster of bare trees. "There's something—" I started to say.

"*Shhh!*" Josh hissed, drawing his sword. Blue fire ignited along its length. "Stay back."

He slid from Honormark's saddle and picked a careful path toward the trees. His steps fell as silently as a cat on the hunt.

Again I found myself wondering how he'd become so brave. What had turned him into a hero?

As Josh drew near, movement erupted in the trees. Long, skeletal branches came to life and reached for him. He dodged this way and that, slashing his sword.

"The trees are attacking him!" Jozlyn cried.

"No, not trees!" I shouted, finally realizing what I should have known all along.

The trees in the small cluster didn't have leaves. They weren't a part of Everleaf Woods. They weren't even real trees.

They were shaddim.

Spinning on the balls of his feet, Josh swatted valiantly at the pack of shaddim. His sword streaked the air with fire.

"Run!" he yelled, but Jozlyn and I were frozen. We couldn't help and we couldn't leave him behind.

We watched the battle in horror. One moment Josh was full of energy and fighting bravely. The next, he fell.

A shaddim snaked out its claws and Josh threw up his sword a fraction of a second too late. Claws brushed his cheek.

"No!" wailed Jozlyn.

Josh collapsed in a heap like a doll dropped from a child's hand. He lay face down in the dirt, and the fire on his sword sizzled out.

Moaning gleefully, the shaddim turned to me.

Ooowhooo-ooh-ooo.

14

Josh didn't move. I couldn't even tell if he was breathing.

"Filthy shaddim!" Jozlyn roared with such force that it startled Chet. I'd never heard her use that tone before—or since, I'm happy to say.

Her eyes blazed with anger as she drew her miniature broom from her satchel. She clutched it in both hands like a weapon and jumped from the saddle.

"No!" I cried. "Don't!" Being brave was one thing. Attacking a pack of shaddim was another.

Jozlyn clearly wasn't thinking straight. Seeing her brother fall must've been more than she could take.

So I did the only thing I could. I attacked. Without a weapon or magic to protect me, I kicked Chet into a charge.

The shaddim saw me coming and moaned louder, hungrily. They sped toward me with their hollow mouths open and their bodies swaying like charmed snakes.

I was sure they wouldn't stop at putting me to sleep. They wanted the Horn and would destroy me to get it.

I raced past Jozlyn and purposefully cut her off. I wanted Chet between her and the shaddim.

Unfortunately, that put me in the middle.

Seeing me coming, the shaddim went berserk. Their moaning droned at an ear-throbbing pitch. Their flaming eyes blazed with excitement.

I threw up my arm—the one wearing Uncle Arick's gauntlet. He'd given it to me for a reason. It was time to find out why.

The shaddim were almost on top of me. They snarled and pawed at one another to be first to reach me, and the putrid stench of their breath blasted my face. Their leader spread its claws, reared back, and—

Krrzzzzt-THOOOM!

A blinding flash struck the shaddim and sent them flying. Dazzling colors whirled and shimmered in a brilliant explosion of light.

When the flash faded, I nearly cheered. The shaddim were scattered and floating as if asleep, bobbing slowly like gentle waves a foot in the air. Their claws scraped the ground.

The cheer stuck in my throat when I saw the source of the light—the gypsy wagon. It had appeared out of nowhere as fast as a bolt of lightning. Steam rose from its silvery wheels.

"Now do no be for running again," the woman with the strange accent said from inside.

15

"Go away!" Jozlyn screeched at the wagon. She was bent over Josh's unmoving body, tugging his shoulders. Trying to drag him toward Everleaf Woods.

The wagon silently ignored her. The floating eyeball hadn't reappeared, and the trapdoor hadn't opened. There was no movement from the shaddim either, except their rhythmic bobbing.

"Jasiah, help me," she requested. "We have to get Josh away from here. He's still breathing!"

Josh was alive! The shaddim had only put him to sleep.

"Hurry, please," Jozlyn pleaded.

"Into the woods?" I asked, scrambling from Chet's saddle. Was Jozlyn still thinking crazy? Everleaf Woods wasn't safe.

She gave me a look that told me she was her usual self. "Yes, the woods. Or would you rather wait for the shaddim to wake up? Or to see what comes out of the wagon next?"

"What about the horses?" I protested. I was trying every excuse I could for not going into the woods.

"Broomstick knows the way home," Jozlyn assured me. "The others will follow her."

I glanced doubtfully at the horses then back at Jozlyn. The horses couldn't follow us into the thick woods, and we couldn't stay in the open. Not with the wagon so close and the shaddim about to wake up.

I threw my arms up helplessly. What choice did we have? Everleaf Woods was our only escape.

After tucking Josh's fallen sword into my belt, Jozlyn and I half-dragged, half-carried Josh into the trees. As we did, the voice from the wagon called out again. "What goes in also makes coming out. Seeing you again, will I."

I tried to ignore the words without much success. We would exit the forest eventually. When we did, the wagon would be waiting for us.

Silence surrounded us as we shuffled into the woods, and our movements and breathing echoed eerily. Black leaves hid the sky, choking out the light, but not a single one lay on the ground. We were alone in a dead world.

"Here," Jozlyn panted, setting Josh's legs down gently. "Fetch me a sturdy vine please."

I didn't ask why. Arguing in the gloomy woods seemed like a bad idea. Even our breathing seemed unwelcome.

Everleaf Woods might have looked dead, but I was sure it

69

was alive. And angry.

Finding a vine was easy. They dangled everywhere like long, hairy spider legs. I half expected them to wiggle when I cut one down with Josh's sword.

"Tie it around his ankle," Jozlyn instructed. "And make sure it's secure."

As I bent to the task, she softly sang another rhyme.

Whispers and wishes
Waft on the breeze.
Flotsam and fishes
Float with such ease.
Soaring is simple—
Swimming in sky.
Now you be nimble,
Nesting on high.

"Ready?" she asked when she'd stopped singing.

"Uh, you bet," I said hesitantly, checking the knot around Josh's leg a final time. Did she expect me to drag him around the woods like a toy wagon?

She didn't explain but knelt down and touched her brother on the forehead with the bristles of her tiny broom. A warm breeze brushed my cheek and ruffled my hair, then Josh started to float. He spun in lazy circles, climbing higher.

"The vine!" Jozlyn cried. "Grab it!"

Coiled next to me, the vine unwound like a snake from a basket. As Josh drifted higher, the vine went with him.

70

I dove forward, both hands grasping. My fingers squeezed and caught—

Nothing but air!

The vine slithered out of my grasp, levitating steadily upward. From my back, I watched Josh rise into the tangled branches overhead and disappear.

16

"What have you done?" I roared at Jozlyn, instantly regretting it. It wasn't her fault that I'd let go of the vine.

"Me?" she exclaimed. "You're the one with butterfingers!"

Not wanting to argue, I slumped to the ground and shook my head bitterly. "You're right. I'm sorry."

Unfortunately, sorry didn't cut it. Josh was floating somewhere over Everleaf Woods. My apology didn't change that.

"I'm sorry, too," Jozlyn said. "I'm sorry we aren't taller."

Taller? "Huh?" I looked up to see her jump at something just out of reach.

It was the end of a vine—Josh's vine. Squinting up, I spotted Josh still asleep and lodged beneath a leafy branch. His vine hung down like the string on a balloon.

I suddenly understood Jozlyn's plan. She hadn't wanted

me to pull Josh like a wagon. She expected me to tug him like a balloon!

I almost laughed. Josh was safe. We just had to get him down. As I stared at him, I wondered what kinds of dreams he was having.

"What about a stick?" I suggested, but Jozlyn shook her head.

"Won't work," she said, jumping again. "We have to pull down on the vine. We can't grip with a stick."

I nodded and looked around for something to stand on. The vine wasn't that far above our heads.

Fallen logs, most rotten and full of creepy insects, lay here and there, but none close to the vine. Moving one would have been near impossible. The trees grew too close together.

The trees! I could climb one. Why hadn't I thought of it sooner?

Now that I had a plan, I didn't like it. Feeling the cold touch of the trees brush against me was creepy enough. Wrapping my arms around one would be disgusting, almost like hugging a corpse.

"I guess I'm going up," I announced with a shudder that I hoped Jozlyn didn't notice.

Her eyes widened in understanding. "Be care..." she started to say then changed her mind. "Don't fall and break your leg, or I'll have to cast a floating spell on you, too."

I tried to smile at her joke up ended up scowling, so I

73

turned my attention to the tree nearest Josh's vine.

Being small and light has advantages. For one, I can climb like a squirrel. At least I'd call that an advantage in most any place but Everleaf Woods.

The tree's bark was rough and lined with deep grooves. Some were so wide that I could fit the toe of my boot between them for extra leverage. My climb was almost easy.

Until the leaves started to fall, that is.

Less that ten feet up, the tree began to quiver. Just a gentle vibration at first, the shaking rapidly increased to a dangerous rumble. Twigs and acorns plopped onto my head and slipped down the back of my cloak.

With my teeth clenched, I ignored them as best I could and whispered quietly to myself. *Just a little farther*, I promised. I was almost level with Josh's vine.

That's when the first leaf struck.

Vzzzt! it darted toward me like an angry bee buzzing noisily. *Sploot!* it slapped wetly onto my bare arm.

"*Bleh!*" I gasped, clawing frantically at the damp leaf. Its touch sent a chill up my arm and felt scratchy like a cat's tongue at the same time.

I peeled it off angrily and threw it down, barely keeping my grip on the tree. To my astonishment, the leaf didn't fall. It looped in a tight arc and headed back toward me.

Horrified, I suddenly understood the secret of Everleaf Woods. The black leaves of its trees could fly. That's why there weren't any on the ground.

Vzzzt!

Suddenly, dozens of leaves joined the first, dropping like hail in a storm. *Vzzzt-sploot!* they slapped onto my skin, my clothes, and my hair.

"Jump!" Jozlyn cried again and again. I could barely hear her over the noise of the falling leaves.

Glancing once at Josh's vine, I held my breath and leaped.

17

"Gotcha!" I grunted as my fingers snagged Josh's vine. Leaves plastered my body like a suit of slimy black armor, but I managed to hold on.

Then I braced for a crash landing that never came.

Instead of dropping like a stone, I drifted slowly to the ground. Josh really was a balloon! Jozlyn met me and helped to rip the leaves from my clothes.

To our relief, the leaves zipped back up into the branches and didn't attack again. I guess they didn't mind us being in the woods to long as we didn't try climbing more trees.

"Hang on to the vine," Jozlyn said, pointing up the floating Josh. "The spell won't wear off until he wakes."

I looped the vine around my wrist several times just to be safe. "Got it. Now let's get away from here."

Jozlyn shrugged. "It's going to be awhile. We back-tracked on the horses. We'll have to watch out for

Croneswart Swamp now."

I almost asked about that but decided against it. Jozlyn seemed familiar with the area. Besides, no swamp could be as dangerous as a woods full of killer trees, could it?

We walked long into the evening, stopping only to untangle Josh when he caught on a low branch. Sap coated his hair and jagged rips streaked his cloak.

Still, it was the easiest way to bring him along. Certainly easier than carrying him. I just wasn't sure Josh would agree once he woke.

When his head bonked on an occasional branch and sent him spinning, I tried hard not to think about it.

Or to laugh.

Darkness fell and we kept walking. Jozlyn didn't admit it, but I think she might have been lost. Either that, or looking for something.

She set a furious pace, slowing only once to cast a globe of light on the whiskers of her tiny broom. She held it above her head like a torch and we plodded on.

Finally, I had to ask. "What is that thing? The broom."

In the dim light, I couldn't be sure, but Jozlyn might have blushed. "Every witch—every enchantress—carries a broom. Just because riding one is silly doesn't mean I don't need it for spells."

She didn't slow down or look at me when she spoke. Her eyes remained fixed on the gloom ahead.

When she splashed into icy water without stopping, I

caught her by the shoulder. "What are you doing? We can't walk through swamp."

Jozlyn glanced down at her feet like she hadn't noticed the water. "Oh, I guess you're right. We should…my friend…."

She never had the chance to finish.

Water and gooey muck exploded in a splattering funnel. Globs of slime hurtled through the air.

Blurp!

In the middle of it all, a jellylike creature rose from the depths of the swamp. As big as an elephant, it reminded me of a lump of chunky pudding that had slopped out of its bowl. It sloshed wildly like the waters of a stormy sea.

Gloo-blup! Blurp! More clumps of goo spewed into the air. They belched from rubbery stalks that sprouted all over the jelly-creature's body like eyes on a potato.

"*Ick!*" Jozlyn gagged, a sour look on her face. "A Jellybelch!"

Ick wasn't the half of it. The Jellybelch was a mountain of stinking ooze.

Peppered with dark spots like hairy fungus, its clear skin was see-through and glistened slimily. Assorted debris floated inside it like pieces of fruit in a holiday dessert— bones, turtle shells, sticks, whole fish, and a bunch of things I couldn't identify.

"Let's get out of here!" I shouted. The Jellybelch was coming closer, looking to add us to the collection of gooey trophies trapped inside it.

Blurp! Gloo-blup! the Jellybelch belched grossly.

I snatched Jozlyn's arm and tugged hard on Josh's vine. It might have been the force of my pull or the belching of the slime, but that's right when Josh awoke.

The vine around my wrist suddenly went slack and Josh tumbled into the swamp, arms flailing. "Help!" he choked, struggling to keep his head above water.

18

Josh floundered in the swamp as the Jellybelch oozed toward him. Globs of goo splattered him, keeping him pinned in the water.

"Jozlyn, make him float again!" I cried. I figured we could worry about getting him down later.

"I can't," she wailed. "I have to be able to touch him."

So much for magic. After all the wonders I'd seen, magic couldn't do everything. *That's why heroes carry swords*, I realized. *For when everything else fails.*

I wasn't a hero, but I did have a sword. Maybe that would count for something.

Screaming at the top of my lungs, I pulled Josh's sword from my belt and sloshed deeper into the swamp. Muck sucked at my boots and waves battered my legs.

Right away, the Jellybelch saw the fire on Josh's blade and changed directions. At least that part of my plan had worked. Josh wasn't its target anymore.

Gloo-blup! Gloo-blup! It hurled its goo.

As I dodged the slimy missiles, it occurred to me that I must have looked pretty heroic. Me, average nobody Jasiah Dragonsbane, charging after a monster with a flaming sword in my hands.

But I didn't feel heroic. I mostly felt scared, and I hoped no one noticed. I didn't want Josh and Jozlyn to tease me later. They were real heroes and probably never got scared.

I awkwardly waved the sword at the Jellybelch. I had no idea what I was doing. A real hero would know how to swing a sword.

Blue flames flickered and spat, and the slime retreated, oozing inward like a chubby man sucking in his stomach. My attack swiped in a clean miss.

Fresh goo-globs blasted me, slapping wetly and covering me with slime. One squished against my forehead like a raw egg and dripped into my eyes. Another splatted onto my sword arm, knocking the weapon from my grasp.

The sword tumbled into the water, hissed, and went out. It sank quickly into the muck and disappeared.

Gloo-blup! Seeing me defenseless, the monster attacked furiously. *Blurp!*

I stumbled blindly, pawing at the goo in my eyes. *Why did I think I could be a hero? Why was I on this quest?* All I'd managed to do was lose Josh's sword and put us all in danger.

Something solid struck my shin, and I went splashing down. Not another slime-missile but an object as hard as rock.

"Or dear! Excuse me, young sir," it apologized. At least that's what it sounded like. But what sort of creature that lived in a swamp would have good manners?

I tried to catch a look at it but couldn't. With the slime in my eyes, the object was nothing more than a roundish, dark shape swimming through the swamp.

Then suddenly, more dark shapes joined it. Much smaller than the first, they swam straight at the Jellybelch. There were dozens of them, maybe hundreds. They swam from every direction.

Leading them in a heroic charge, the big shape sang an odd battle cry.

From the dark and the damp
Of Croneswart Swamp
My friends need our help!

Finally, I scooped the goop from my eyes and stared at the singing creature. My jaw dropped.

The polite singer was the biggest turtle I'd ever seen in my life.

Turtlecraft Crunch

19

Turtles of every shaped flooded the swamp. Snapping turtles, horned turtles, turtles with flippers and turtles with fins.

"Turtlecraft Crunch!" crowed the leader. "Give him shell!"

As one, the turtles lowered their heads and charged. The Jellybelch flung its goop at them but it splashed harmlessly on their shells.

Bloof! Bliff! Bloing! The turtles rammed the Jellybelch. Water churned in white, frothy swirls and the monster's stalks flailed helplessly.

For all its size and endless supply of goo, the Jellybelch wasn't a match for the turtle army. With a final, noisy burp, it gave up and sank into the swamp, melting away like warm ice cream.

"Gramble!" Jozlyn exclaimed, half crying and half

cheering. She ran into the water and threw her arms around the big turtle's neck.

By big, I mean really big. The turtle was probably five feet across.

"Hmm, hello, Miss Jozlyn," Gramble the turtle replied in a slow, deep voice. "What a pleasure to see you again." The turtle smiled.

"Hi, Gramble," Josh said, dripping wet from head to toe.

"Ah, and Master Josh, too," Gramble drawled. "Greetings, greetings. But who, may I ask, is your new friend?"

I realized Gramble meant me. He'd obviously met Josh and Jozlyn before. "I'm Jasiah. Uh, it's nice to meet you." I felt silly doing it, but I bowed to the turtle.

"Another polite young fellow," Gramble said. "On behalf of turtles and rocks everywhere, I welcome you to Croneswart Swamp, sir."

I bowed again, not knowing how else to respond.

"Gramble, we need to get across the swamp," Jozlyn interjected hurriedly. "Would you please give us a ride?"

I blinked in surprise. It was one thing to meet a talking turtle. It was another to ask him for a ride.

But Gramble didn't seem to mind. "Certainly. Hmm, that is, I will be honored to serve in that capacity. Please climb aboard."

Josh and Jozlyn nearly jumped onto Gramble's broad shell. I stepped on cautiously, afraid I'd squish Gramble or make a fool of myself by slipping into the water.

I did neither, and we were quickly on our way.

Jozlyn used a spell to dry us off then spoke quietly with Gramble, laughing and smiling. Not wanting to eavesdrop, I described to Josh everything that had happened since he'd fallen asleep.

"Good thing Gramble showed up," he said when I'd finished. "I wasn't any help splashing around in the water."

I grinned, too, feeling better and safer than I had since beginning our quest. "And when I lost your sword, I thought…."

My sentence drifted off, swallowed by a knot in my stomach. "Your sword!" I gasped. "It's at the bottom of the swamp!"

Josh calmly patted his hip and smiled. His sword was in its sheath. "You were busy crying, so I got it," he said with a straight face.

"Crying! I had goo in my eyes!" I protested.

"Sure, blame it on that," he laughed, winking, and I realized that he was teasing me.

I bugged my eyes at him. "At least I didn't take a nap, balloon-boy."

Josh opened his mouth to say something but no words came out. We both laughed. We'd had quite a day.

Not long after, Gramble landed on a tiny round island that rose out of the swamp like a hill. It sloped gently upward and was covered with soft, dry swamp grass.

"I suspect that even brave heroes require slumber," the

turtle stated, "and it is quite late. Please take respite here. I shall act as your aquatic sentry until morning."

It took me a minute to realize that Gramble meant for us to sleep while he kept watch.

"But what about you?" Jozlyn asked. "Don't you need rest?"

Gramble smiled sadly at her, and his eyes shined brightly. "Not this eve, Miss Jozlyn. Hmm, I intend to enjoy and remember every moment of this night as if it were my last."

His words hinted at something but he didn't say more, and we didn't pry. Still, as I drifted off to sleep, I wondered what would make a turtle believe he didn't have long to live.

Gramble's Goodbye

20

Very early in the morning, I woke to Jozlyn and Gramble arguing in hushed tones. Again, I didn't want to eavesdrop, but interrupting would have been even more impolite.

"…No, no, no," Jozlyn was saying, "I won't do it. How can you even ask?"

Gramble sighed a slow rumble. "It is the way of things, Miss Jozlyn. The *proper* way. I appreciate your gift but it was not intended to endure indefinitely."

"But—" Jozlyn began before a hearty sob cut her off. She cried softly for awhile. "I'll miss you," she finally wailed.

"Hmm, oh my," Gramble drawled. "As will I miss you, lass. But I miss my other friends now. I cannot hear their deep, soothing voices. Their songs are lost to me."

Jozlyn didn't respond for a long time. She wept quietly, her face pressed against the turtle's long neck. At last she whispered, "Alright, Gramble, alright. I'll do it."

We departed soon after. No one spoke or laughed. Only Jozlyn's occasional sniff intruded on our silence.

Bobbing along on Gramble's shell, we nibbled a breakfast taken from Dreamsafe Den, but I barely tasted any of it. The tension between Jozlyn and Gramble cast a dark mood over everything.

When land appeared out of the fog, I was more than happy to leave Croneswart Swamp behind. But only if we'd lost the shaddim would our detour have been worth the trouble.

I hoped we'd escaped the strange gypsy wagon, too, but remembered the woman's words. *What goes in also makes coming out. Seeing you again, will I*, she'd told us.

On the shore, Gramble shuffled here and there. He finally settled on a narrow peninsula that extended into the water and was covered with grass. On sunny days, the peninsula would be warm and cozy.

Josh patted the turtle's head then backed off the peninsula. "Goodbye, Gramble, and thank you for everything." There might have been a tear in his eye.

"Farewell, Master Josh," Gramble replied. "I will always remember your courage and friendship."

Jozlyn went to the turtle next. She knelt before him, whispered, hugged his neck, and then sang a quiet song.

Pebbles, rocks, and boulder blocks
Sing songs strong and true.
Join them, friend, make turtle's end—
Take our tunes with you.

She dabbed Gramble lightly on the nose with her minia-ture broom, and he started to change. His shell expanded, stretching to cover his limbs.

"Thank you, Miss Jozlyn, thank you," he said, his deep voice sounding farther and farther away. "I have experienced…two lives. You…best of friends…turtle… rock…."

His final words were lost as his shell surrounded him. There was a soft flash of light, and then Gramble was no more. A large, spotted rock rested on the peninsula where he'd been.

"Goodbye, Gramble Turtlecraft Extraordinaire," Jozlyn whispered before joining us on the shore. Tears streamed down her cheeks.

"Jozlyn, I'm—" Josh began but Jozlyn waved her hand.

"Just go," she sniffed. "Go, please. We have to find the Horn. I'll be all right." As if to prove it, she started walk-ing and left us staring after her.

I moved to catch up but Josh caught my arm. "Listen, Jasiah. Jozlyn turned Gramble into a turtle over a year ago," he explained. "He really is supposed to be a rock."

Josh said it like he needed to apologize, but I understood.

I'd heard Gramble talking. He'd wanted Jozlyn to change him back.

I nodded and forced a smile. "We'd better not let her get too far ahead."

We caught her at the edge of the trees where Everleaf Woods and Croneswart Swamp gave way to wide, open grasslands. She'd stopped to gawk at something, one hand covering her mouth.

The *something* was the gypsy wagon. It rolled to a stop on a short hill directly in front of us.

Jozlyn sniffed once more and took a deep breath. "That's it," she said with fierce determination. "I'm going to find out what this is all about."

Arms pumping, she set off toward the wagon.

One Eyed Stare

21

Sword in hand, Josh started after his sister. He knew better than to argue. Jozlyn was already upset. If she wanted to see who was in the gypsy wagon, that's exactly what we'd do.

I knew better than to argue, too. We'd made it through Everleaf Woods and Croneswart Swamp because of Jozlyn. I trusted her.

We approached the rear of the wagon. Two bright orange swinging doors blocked our view of the inside. Neither was locked.

"I'll go first," Josh offered. "You two be ready if there's trouble."

Once again, I marveled at him. He was ready to face new danger even after being put to sleep by shaddim and being dragged around like a balloon.

I'll never be that brave, I thought. Josh was only two

years older than me but the difference seemed like twenty.

Jozlyn shook her head at her brother. "No," she disagreed, "we have to go together. The last time we split up...."

She didn't finish her sentence because Josh and I knew what she meant. When Josh had gone off alone the last time, the shaddim had attacked. We couldn't risk being separated again.

"Alright, then, on three," Josh said, still refusing to argue. He gripped the swinging doors, one in each hand, and took a deep breath. "One...two...three!"

On *three*, he threw the doors wide and they clattered against the sides of the wagon. Sparkling light filled with twinkling bits like stardust poured out from inside.

"What's in there?" Jozlyn asked, squinting into the light.

I swiped at the sparkles as if they were gnats. "I don't know. I can't—"

The woman with the accent interrupted me. "Ahh, at last my young friends have made deciding to visit."

Jozlyn raised her broom defensively. "*Y*-yes, we have. But not until you show yourself."

A slim shadow appeared in the light, moving forward slowly. To my relief, it had a human shape, not the wispy curves of a shaddim.

A throaty cackle drifted from the wagon. Even the woman's laugh had an accent!

"Aye, you have," the woman laughed cheerfully. "Being

93

glad for that I am."

We held our breath as the shadow took shape. Josh crouched in a warrior's pose, and Jozlyn clutched her broom in both hands. Not having a weapon, I gripped our piece of the Dragonsbane Horn. I'd hung it from my belt like a sword.

The three of us expected a monster or another floating eyeball. Anything but—

A beautiful woman?

The light faded and the sparkles winked into nothingness. From the wagon stepped a slender woman with smooth brown skin. She seemed to glide rather than walk.

Dressed in a long flowing skirt and blouse, the woman spread her arms in greeting. Colorful silk scarves fluttered gently behind her, and polished bracelets tinkled musically from her wrists and forearms.

"Welcoming you I am to my vardo," she said with a broad smile on her ruby lips. "I am being Medium Mirelda."

The painted words on the side of the wagon finally made sense. *Medium Mirelda's Volacious Vardo*. Mirelda was the owner of the wagon.

"Hi, I'm Ja—" I started to say when Josh grabbed my shoulder and yanked me back a step.

"What do you want with us?" he demanded.

Mirelda cocked an eye at him. *One* eye. Her left eye stared at me, and her right squinted at Josh.

My knees trembled at the bizarre sight. Her eyes were focused in two different directions! How could they do that?

"Asking what *you* want of Mirelda is better question, Josh Vinerider, Deputy of Tiller's Field," she stated.

"How do…my name?" Josh mumbled in surprise.

Mirelda blinked slowly, ignoring him. When she opened her eyes, they were both looking forward and straight at me.

"Jasiah Dragonsbane has a wanting for answers," she purred. "Let him speak the asking of your quest."

I gulped in alarm, and my hands felt suddenly clammy. The Horn slipped from my fingers.

How did Mirelda know our names and about our quest? Except for us, only Wizard Ast and Uncle Arick were supposed to know about it.

I glanced thoughtfully at the Horn and then back to Mirelda. She had answers, I realized without knowing how. She knew all about us and the Dragonsbane Horn.

Swallowing hard, I tried to find my courage. "Where do we find the next piece of the Horn?" I asked quietly.

Mirelda smiled and her right eye rolled unpleasantly in its socket. "I felt afraid you would never be asking," she said mysteriously. "Let me be telling you."

22

"Make coming inside now," Medium Mirelda said. "Sharing secrets is quiet business." She gestured at the wagon with one hand, her bracelets clinking like wind chimes.

Josh stepped inside first, Jozlyn and I on his heels. None of us wanted to be left alone with Mirelda. Her silken scarves *swished* as she tugged the doors closed.

Darkness filled the wagon, and I couldn't see a thing. Not Josh or Jozlyn. Not the doors we'd just used. My heart beat faster and I started to gasp for breath.

"*C*-can we have some light, please?" I asked, trying to stay calm. My imagination was running wild in the darkness.

Mirelda's rich cackled tickled my ears but not from behind me where it should have been. Somehow, she'd slipped past me.

A green spark warmed into a soft glow ahead of me, and I concentrated on it, thankful for any light. As it brightened, I spotted Mirelda sitting at a tiny round table, the glowing light swirling on her palm.

The light expanded, and its cheery glow spread throughout the wagon. In seconds, the glow was a spinning ball the size of a cantaloupe.

Staring at the light didn't hurt my eyes, and I noticed that it was covered with colorful pictures. Tiny mountains, forests, rivers, and more spread across its surface. I even thought I could see a miniature Everleaf Woods.

The ball, I realized, was a globe of the world.

"You wish to be finding the Horn of Dragonsbane," Mirelda said, one eye on the globe and one on us. I wanted to shudder under that creepy gaze but forced myself to hold still.

"But you are not knowing where for to search," she added.

"That's not quite true," Jozlyn protested. "Jasiah decided that the next piece is in Silvermight. We're on our way there."

Jasiah decided? I shot Jozlyn a look but didn't say anything. We'd agreed together that Silvermight was where we needed to look.

"We shall be seeing, then," Mirelda whispered, "if your guessing is right."

She placed the globe atop a brass dish on the table and

closed her eyes. The globe's images faded, and its surface turned milky white.

"What's she…?" I began when Jozlyn cut me off by stepping firmly on my foot.

"It's magic, ninny," she huffed. "Don't you know what a *medium* is? Mirelda's a fortune-teller."

"Oh," I said flatly, dislodging my foot. I wasn't about to admit that I hadn't known what a medium was. I'd halfway thought that Mirelda was a middle sister. Being in the middle, she was medium.

Mirelda cradled the globe in both hands like it was a precious treasure. When she opened her eyes, they were glazed and milky like the globe. In her thick accent, she chanted.

In sand with skulls
And shattered hulls,
The doom of dragons seek.

Set prow to ply
For pirate's eye
'Tween main and mountain peak.

'Ware weirds and wards
Of swallowed hoards
Where greedy gluttons speak.

Trust dwarves who dare
With dauntless flair.
Their ships and souls aren't weak.

Pictures formed in my mind as she chanted. I saw ship-wrecks, oceans of sand, and dwarven sailors searching for their lost home. When the words ended, the images disappeared.

"Silvermight," I whispered, more convinced than ever. Where else would we find dwarven ships sailing through sand between mountains?

Medium Mirelda's fortune hadn't told us anything new, I realized with disappointment. But it had confirmed our thoughts. The next piece of the Horn was in Silvermight.

"What do you think it means, lady?" Jozlyn asked. "Did the fortune describe the lost city of Silvermight?"

Mirelda released the globe and blinked the milky film from her eyes. "You must be deciding that, just as you made deciding to visit. Spoiling the fortune would my help do."

I understood what she meant right away. Mirelda *saw* the future. She didn't *control* it. If she interfered with a fortune, it wouldn't come true.

"That's why you followed us but didn't invite us inside," Josh said, figuring out the same thing I had. "We had to come to you."

Mirelda smiled and nodded. "Truth," she agreed, "though please to accept my apology for making a scare."

Jozlyn shrugged politely. "It's alright. I understand magic."

On the other side of her, Josh groaned. "Oh sure, after she explains it, you understand." I couldn't see him do it, but I was sure he rolled his eyes.

Jozlyn sucked in a deep breath, preparing to lecture her brother. Mirelda cleared her throat before Jozlyn had the chance.

The fortune-teller faced us, one arm cocked in front of her chest. Balanced delicately on the tip of her index finger, the globe rotated slowly. Lakes, cities, trees, and islands spun in and out of view.

"Now be showing," Mirelda invited, "where you wish for to go."

23

I stared in confusion at the spinning globe on Mirelda's fingertip. What was I supposed to do with it?

"Touch it," Jozlyn whispered into my ear, answering my silent question.

Touch it? Still confused, I glanced at her. "Where?"

Jozlyn made a face like I was missing something that she could see with her eyes closed. "Wherever you want to go," she said impatiently.

I thought about that a while. Where did I really want to go? To Silvermight in search of the Horn? To Tiller's Field in hopes of finding Uncle Arick and Kadze? Back home— where?

Finally I decided that I didn't have a choice. Not a real one anyway. I was on a quest. Until it was over, family, friends, and whatever I might want would have to wait.

Making decisions, I realized, was part of being a hero.

Decisions I might not like but that helped others. I didn't have a magic sword or a book of spells, but I could still do my part.

I felt pretty good about that.

With one finger, I reached out and stopped the globe from spinning. My fingertip covered the picture of a town and sailing ship on the eastern edge of the Sandy Sea.

"There," I said, louder than I'd intended. "I want to go there."

If Silvermight was lost in the Sandy Sea like the legends claimed, we'd need a ship to find it. How ships sailed across sand, I couldn't imagine.

"Prospect Peak," Mirelda said, and I guessed that was the name of the town under my finger. I knew as much about that area as I did about sailing in sand.

I tried to ask about Prospect Peak, but a sudden jerk sucked the air from my lungs. The wagon trembled beneath my feet and knocked me to the floor. Jozlyn and Josh tumbled down on top of me.

"What's happening?" Josh cried as we tried to untangle ourselves.

"My volacious vardo," Mirelda beamed, "is making for the Dragonsbane's destination. Be hanging onto your stomachs!"

Sure enough, the wagon rumbled and shook as if pulled by a team of galloping unicorns. My stomach flopped with every bounce. It might have been fun if the wagon didn't feel like it was going to shake itself apart.

Mirelda swayed in her seat as calmly as a ship's captain in a hammock. The rest of us scrambled to a wall and hung on for dear life.

"It's...the...globe," Jozlyn gasped between bounces. "It makes...the wagon move."

I nodded at her with a grimace on my face. When I'd wondered how the wagon moved without horses to pull it, I'd known magic was responsible. Finding out just how right I'd been didn't make my stomach feel any better.

But it did explain how the wagon had stayed ahead of us. Mirelda had touched the globe and sent the wagon zooming. It had been impossible for us to outrun it.

Krrzzzzt-THOOOM!

The same explosion we'd heard when the wagon had crashed into the shaddim boomed in our ears. At first I thought the roof had blow off, but the wagon jerked to a safe stop in one piece.

"Why are we stopping?" I asked. I wasn't disappointed, just curious.

Mirelda didn't answer right away. She stood, smoothed her clothes, and patted her hair. Finally, she smiled.

"Be enjoying your visit to Prospect Peak," she said, "and not forgetting my words."

A creaking behind us caused me to turn my head. As I did, my ears felt plugged like I had a cold, or like we were somewhere very high up.

The wagon's doors opened. Outside, golden mountain peaks rose like a wall of dragon's teeth. Sand and more sand clung to their sides and blanketed the ground like snow.

The Glittersgold Mountains and the Sandy Sea! In just hours aboard Mirelda's wagon, we'd magically traveled across the grasslands. The journey would have taken us days on horseback.

I wiggled my jaw to pop my ears. When they did, I heard Jozlyn whisper.

One sounds in the sands
Of the dwarven home.

We were getting closer to finding the second piece of the Dragonsbane Horn.

Eye Scout

24

The Glittersgold Mountains sparkled like jewels as the sun set behind them. The sight was breath-taking, and I understood immediately where the mountains had gotten their name.

But it was the sand that caught my eye. Rolling just like an ocean, it filled a great bowl-shaped valley that seemed to have been pulverized by a giant fist. The mountains of the valley were gone, leaving only sand to mark where they'd been.

"We'll never find anything in that," I mumbled hope-lessly. The sand stretched on forever. Finding a needle in a haystack would be easier!

Where had so much sand come from anyway, and where had the mountains gone? As I gazed at the Sandy Sea, I doubted I'd ever know the answers to my questions. Others had been trying to solve the same riddles for centuries.

"Be standing back," Mirelda requested, interrupting my dreary thoughts. "I will make a scouting for danger."

To my astonishment, she reached over her shoulder and smacked herself soundly on the back of the head.

Squickt!

With a horrible, squishy pop, her right eye squirted out of its socket and hung in the air in front of her face. It rotated once in a full circle then zipped out of the wagon. The familiar mosquito buzzing went with it.

"Gross!" Jozlyn gagged, covering her own eyes. "I'd rather kiss a frog!" Which she'd done, I found out.

Even Josh's faced turned white.

But Mirelda didn't look concerned. She faced the doors and pressed her lips together in thought. Thankfully she kept her right eyelid squeezed shut. I don't think I could have looked at her otherwise.

The eyeball returned shortly. "I was spotting no danger," Mirelda reported. "Many boats. No lobsterpods. The path for going into town is safe."

She caught the eyeball and casually wiped it on her skirt the way a person cleans the dirty lens in a pair of spec-tacles. When she raised her arm, I looked away.

Squooch!

The wet sound of the eyeball fitting back into place left me weak in the knees.

"Be making haste before nightfall," Mirelda advised. "Darkness is no for children in a pirate's playground."

Josh's head came up sharply. "Pirates?"

Mirelda cocked her head at him. "In places having silver and lost treasure, pirates always are making business."

I shivered at the truth of her words. I should have thought of pirates sooner. A sea, ships, dwarven treasure. Of course there'd be pirates.

Hadn't Mirelda's fortune even mentioned them? Something about a pirate's eye, I think it was.

As we said goodbye to Mirelda, I wondered about pirates and their eyes. Was Mirelda more than a fortune-teller? Was she also a pirate? She had the strangest eye I'd ever seen.

The three of us followed a sandy path between rocks up to the dusty town of Prospect Peak. It wasn't so much a town as a shabby cluster of run-down buildings. A long, crooked pier stretched into the Sandy Sea and was surrounded by boats of all kinds.

"Let's find somewhere to spend the night," Jozlyn suggested.

"And to eat," Josh added. Like me, he was tired of fruit and nuts we'd taken from Dreamsafe Den.

Jozlyn sniffed at him and wrinkled her nose. "Maybe a bath, too. You still smell like a Jellybelch."

The two of them started arguing, and I knew better than to get involved. I turned my attention to a man down the street who was having an argument of his own. Strangely, he seemed all alone.

"Shahsah, get back here this instant!" he hissed with a stomp of his foot. He barely paused before repeating his demand more loudly.

Maybe he's calling his pet, I thought. *A cat or dog*. The edge of the street was crowded with barrels and crates. There were dozens of places to hide.

Thinking to help the man, I started to wander down the street, peeking in shadows and under abandoned wagons. Anything was better than listening to Jozlyn and Josh.

"Shahsah, if you don't—*ahh*, there you are!" the man said, his tone changing in mid-sentence.

I glanced up to find him staring straight at me. But that wasn't right. I wasn't a playful puppy.

I turned around and immediately wished I hadn't.

A huge creature floated a few feet away, coming closer. Seemingly made of purple fog, it had thick arms and a broad chest but no legs or hands. Looking at it was like looking at something that wasn't there. I could see right through its misty body.

It floated ahead without glancing at me, and I threw up my arms. It was going to plow into me.

At the last second, I screamed.

25

The foggy, purple creature never slowed. It swept forward like a cloud blown by the wind, blind to whatever lay in its path.

Too bad I was in that path!

Still screaming, I threw myself to the sandy street. Hot air blasted me, throwing up a cloud of dust, and a tingling sensation shot through my body.

I opened my eyes to see the creature on top of me. Its misty torso brushed against my chest and—

Passed right through me.

A ghost! The creature could float through walls—and people. I closed my eyes and screamed again.

"Jasiah! Jasiah!" Josh shouted. "You're alright. It's gone. Get up." Hands clutched my shoulders and shook me until I opened my eyes.

He and Jozlyn crouched over me, their faces concerned.

"That's one way to make us stop arguing," Jozlyn said.

I smiled weakly at her. I would have preferred the argument.

"Ya ain't from aroun' here, is ya?" the man from the street called. I climbed to my feet, and we all looked at him.

"Pardon me?" Jozlyn asked cautiously. Mirelda had warned us about strangers. Any one of them could be a pirate.

The man grinned at us, showing rows of black and missing teeth. He sure looked like a pirate. In one hand he gripped a large bottle made of smoky glass. The purple creature was nowhere to be seen.

"Ya best git to the Last Hope 'fore it gits dark, little ones," he said, still grinning. I didn't like that look one bit.

"Is that an inn—the Last Hope?" Josh asked.

"Sure is. Only one in town. It's back that way, 'round the bend." He waved a dirty hand, indicating the way we'd come.

We turned and fled without a thank you or goodbye. None of us trusted the toothless man, pirate or not.

The Last Hope Inn was even more broken-down than the other buildings in Prospect Peak. Grimy stains covered its walls, and its door was chipped and cut as if it had been hacked by an axe more than once.

"Maybe we should find somewhere else," Jozlyn suggested after taking a look at the inn.

"You heard the man," Josh replied. "This is the only place. Besides, it's almost dark. We can't stay in the streets."

Jozlyn frowned. "I still don't like it," she admitted, and I couldn't help agreeing with her. "So much for your bath."

Josh smirked and reached for the door.

THWONK!

Before he grasped the handle, the door burst open, banging loudly against the outer wall. Three snarling men squeezed through the doorway. The largest dragged the other two by their ears.

"Settle it outside, mates," the big man roared. "No sense bustin' up the place."

Only then did he seem to see us. Or more importantly, to see Josh.

"Well, what've we got 'ere?" he bellowed, twisting the other men's ears so that they were forced to look at Josh, too. "Seems like we gots us a real deputy to settle yer differences."

Josh's deputy's badge! He wore it pinned to his doublet.

"Invite 'em inside, mates!"

The three men reached for us with their big, grimy hands.

26

The three sweaty men dragged us into the Last Hope Inn. By the looks of them, I knew they were pirates. The big one had even called the others *mates*.

That was a pirate word if I ever heard one.

Contrary to its name, the inn didn't offer us any hope. Rough-looking men and women crowded cluttered tables, playing cards or games of dice. Their dark eyes watched us the way mice watch cheese.

The big man snatched a wooden mug and rapped it solidly against a tabletop. The noise was sharp and demanded attention. Slowly the dark eyes shifted from us to him.

"Listen up, mates," he boomed, climbing onto the table so that he could be seen by all. "There's a deputy here to keep us honest. Ain't that right, mate?"

The pirate nodded to one of his companions who shoved

Josh in the back and sent him sprawling. Caught by surprise, Josh flailed his arms and stumbled but managed to catch himself before falling.

Still, laughter erupted throughout the room. "Dance s'more, boy!" called a voice from the back.

Josh hung his head, and I was afraid that he was crying. What could be worse than crying in front of a roomful of pirates? He'd never live it down.

But I couldn't blame him either. These pirates were worse than shaddim. They were people behaving like monsters.

"Leave him alone!" Jozlyn demanded, struggling in the clutches of her pirate captor. More laughter drowned out her words.

In the commotion, Josh sprang into action. He hadn't been crying after all. Just waiting for the right moment.

He whirled to face the big pirate on the table, and ripped his sword from its sheath. When blue fire erupted along the blade, the laughter in the room died and was replaced by a startled gasp.

Josh didn't stop there. He leaped onto his knees, sliding forward, and drew back his arms for a two-handed slash.

Was he going to attack the pirates? It was a gruesome thought. The pirates might be acting like monsters but they were still human.

"Josh, no!" I cried.

Gzzzt-gz-gzk!

Too late. Crackling and sparking, his sword slashed through the air.

The flaming blade bit into the leg of the table the big pirate stood on and sliced clean through the wood.

CRRRAONK!

The table and pirate tumbled over.

Josh jumped to his feet, ready for the worst. He spun lightly on his feet, and waited for the pirates to attack.

They never did. Astonished silence filled the room. Not even the big pirate moved.

Then finally, a man clapped very slowly and loudly. Once, twice, and then three times.

"That was quite a performance, boy," the clapper said. He strode toward Josh with a smirk on his face. What brings ye to Prospect Peak?"

Josh lowered his sword but didn't sheath it. The clapper was obviously an important pirate, probably a captain. He wore polished jewelry on his fingers, in his ears, and around his neck.

Uncomfortable seconds passed before Josh replied. "Silvermight," he said at last, and I breathed a sigh of relief. I was glad he hadn't given away our quest.

The pirate captain chuckled dryly. "Ain't much left of Silvermight. Nothin' but trouble."

Josh ignored the warning. "So you know where it is and can take us there?"

The captain's smirk turned into a greedy smile. "Aye,

that I can," he said, licking his lips, "for a fee. Everything has its price."

From the shadows in the back of the room, a new voice called out. "For a fee, you can sail with me!"

Suddenly, hoots and laughter filled the room. The pirates jumped up and started to stomp their feet, clap, and sing.

Sail with me
Through the Sandy Sea.
For a fee
You can sail with me.

Pay your gold
And passage is sold.
Pack the hold
With silver and gold.

Hoist the sails
For Silvermight's trail.
Hear that gale
Blowing in our sails.

Swab the deck.
Mop up ev'ry speck.
Double-check
Or you'll sleep on deck.

Yo-ho-ho
An' a-*arh, arh, arh*.
Ahoy, matey,
Sail with me

Try to swim!
Outlook's grim.
You can't swim.

It's too late!
Sinking fate—
You're shark bait.

Sail with me
Through the Sandy Sea.
For a fee
You can sail with me.

If we wreck
On our sandy trek,
It's your neck.
Pray we don't shipwreck.

Yo-ho-ho
An' a-*arh, arh, arh.*
Ahoy, matey,
Sail with me

I got the impression that the pirates liked the idea of everything having its price. I could also tell that they'd sung their song before.

It didn't end for a long time, and the pirates seemed especially fond of the part about shark bait. They sang the verse again and again. Some even pointed at us and made cutting gestures across their throats as they sang.

When the song finally died down, the captain stretched

out a jeweled hand. "Yer fee, if ye please, boy. We'll be leavin' for Silvermight at dawn."

Hello Silver, Goodbye Gold

27

The captain's hand twitched eagerly. "Voyage to Silvermight is four gold crowns," he said with his greedy grin. "Payment due—*now*."

Jozlyn sighed but counted the coins onto his open palm. Before leaving Tiller's Field, Wizard Ast had given her five. The fee didn't leave us with much.

The captain snapped his hand closed. "My ship is the *Lawless*. She's moored at the farthest end of the pier." With that, he turned sharply on his heels and strode off.

I stared at his back, thinking dark thoughts and feeling uneasy. We'd given our money to a pirate. Could we trust him?

I almost said something aloud but caught myself. *Of course he can't be trusted*, I huffed silently. *He's a pirate. Look at the name of his ship—the* Lawless*!*

Then I realized the captain hadn't told us *his* name, and I felt worse. Our voyage wasn't off to a good start.

We paid the innkeeper the last of our gold for dinner and a room. Thankfully, he didn't ask our names or ages. I suppose living near pirates had taught him not to be curious about other people's business.

We ate in our room with the door locked and talked deep into the night. We felt too nervous and excited to sleep. Silvermight and the next piece of the Dragonsbane Horn were near.

Personally, I was more nervous than excited. Josh and Jozlyn might've been used to adventures, but I wasn't. I'd never run from monsters, met pirates and talking turtles, or had magic cast on me before. I was afraid I wasn't the hero type.

Jozlyn had already used her magic more than once to save us. Josh had faced off against shaddim and pirates. What had I done?

The answer was a big, fat *nothing*.

I hadn't done anything special, not like you'd expect from the leader of a quest. Wizard Ast would probably regret naming me leader. Uncle Arick….

Uncle Arick would be disappointed. Knowing that was worse than anything we'd faced. *This quest is about you*, he'd said, and that meant something important. But I hadn't been able to figure out what or why.

I hadn't even figured out what to do with his gauntlet! Was it just a piece of armor? Could it cast magic or give

120

me superhuman strength?

So far, all it had done was itch. I couldn't take it off, and I couldn't squeeze my other hand inside it. I'd even tried sticking my dinner fork down in it to get at the itch. Nothing worked.

I finally fell asleep confused, feeling sorry for myself, and itching like crazy.

"Jasiah," Jozlyn called from somewhere beyond my dreams, and I woke to the scent of fried eggs and warm, buttered biscuits.

She and Josh were already up, empty breakfast plates in their hands. A full plate waited on the foot of my bed.

"We let you sleep," Jozlyn said, "but we need to hurry now. It's almost dawn." Outside our window, streaks of orange and red tinted the clouds.

What was that old saying? *Red skies at night, a sailor's delight. Red skies in morn, sailor be warned.*

It hadn't meant anything to me before, but on the day I was to sail with pirates, it gave me feeling of dread.

I sighed and quickly sat up, turning to my breakfast. I wasn't very hungry, not after Jozlyn's words. *We let you sleep* meant that she and Josh had decided I needed looking after.

I was the baby of the quest, the youngest, and the two of them were my babysitters. I was just tagging along.

We left the Last Hope and hurried to find the *Lawless*. The streets of Prospect Peak were fairly empty and quiet, but not the pier. Stepping onto it was like walking into a new world.

People mobbed its entire length. They pushed carts and pulled donkeys. They loaded crates, mopped decks, hoisted sails, and climbed the riggings of their tall ships.

"Raise the anchor!" ordered a captain. "Aye, aye, ma'am!" her crew saluted.

"Trim the sails!"

"Cast off the lines!"

"Lower the jib!"

Shouts and the sounds of labor created a deafening buzz. Jozlyn, Josh, and I almost had to shout to be heard.

"The *Lawless* is supposed to be at the end of the pier," Josh reminded. "Stay close to me."

He put his head down and pushed through the crowd. Men and women grumbled at him, but they grumbled at anyone that came too close. I don't think it was Josh they disliked in particular.

We stopped at the edge of the pier.

"Do you see it?" Josh asked, scanning the assortment of nearby ships.

I shook my head. None of the ships bore the name *Lawless*. I saw the *Fool's Gold*, *Sea Far II*, *Errant*, and *Finder's Keepers*. No *Lawless*.

"It's got to be—*oof*!" Something solid bumped into my back, nearly knocking me into the sand.

I turned to see a short, stocky man with a wild red beard.

He was an adult but not much taller than me. His shoulders and chest were almost as wide as he was tall, and his powerful limbs reminded me of tree trunks.

"A dwarf!" I gasped in astonishment, probably not the most polite thing to do. I hadn't shouted "human!" when I'd met Medium Mirelda.

The dwarf smiled hugely, and I gasped again. His teeth were solid silver! They looked like he'd brushed them with shiny, silver paint.

He noticed me staring and chuckled without moving his jaw. His eyebrows arched in an insane expression. "*Heh-heh-hah-hah-hahgh*!"

How peculiar! Was his mouth welded shut?

Jozlyn curtsied to the dwarf. "Excuse me, sir, but could you tell us where we might find the *Lawless*?"

The dwarf laughed again, this time with a shrug. He pointed a thick finger toward the horizon.

There, I spotted a ship I hadn't noticed. I squinted at it, just making out a name painted on its stern.

The *Lawless*.

The pirates had sailed off with our gold.

Trust Dwarves Who Dare

28

"Can you read the name?" Josh asked, tugging frantically on my arm. "Is that the *Lawless*?"

Watching the pirate ship sail away, I'd forgotten that I could see farther than he and Jozlyn. Farther than most anyone.

I nodded without turning, too disappointed to speak. We'd been tricked. The pirates had taken our gold and left without us.

What were we going to do? We'd come so far, yet Silvermight and the next piece of the Horn had never seemed farther away.

Our quest was hopeless.

Josh threw up his arms. "I knew it! We should've never trusted those pirates."

He knew it, and Jozlyn and I knew it. Pirates were greedy and selfish. Common sense should have told us that.

Jozlyn worked her way to the end of the pier. "Maybe we could swim…or use a spell," she mumbled, mostly to herself.

"Swim?" boomed a large voice. "Not if ye enjoy breathin'. The lobsterpods'd have ye 'fore both feet hit the sand."

Lobsterpods? That name sounded familiar.

A second dwarf joined the first. He was slightly taller and wore a knotted silver diadem on his bald head. His long auburn beard was carefully braided, and his teeth were white.

"Captain Truebold here, skipper o' the *Errant*," he greeted us. "This be me first mate, Grinshine. Don't let his fearsome teeth scare ye, he don't bite." He shared a wink with the other dwarf. "He can't open his mouth!"

Grinshine chuckled with that crazy look on his face. "*Heh-heh-hah-har-hargh.*"

Then Captain Truebold added, "Can we be of assistance?"

I knew right away that these men weren't pirates. Maybe it was their smiles—even Grinshine's silver smile—or our urgent need for help, but I felt I could trust them.

"We need to get to Silvermight," I admitted.

Captain Truebold tugged on a fistful of his beard. "Yer in luck then. So do we," he said. "Are ye ready to leave? Our efreet is tuggin' on its lines."

125

He stabbed a stubby finger at a beautiful ship. Rich, polished wood and gold-white sails made it a jewel among the shabby pirate ships with skull-stitched flags.

"Finest ship on the Sandy Sea," Truebold added proudly.

Jozlyn wasn't convinced. She pointed a shaky finger into the air. "What's that thing?"

Floating in front of the *Errant* was one of the massive purple creatures we'd seen the night before. It wore a chain harness over its misty shoulders that trailed down to the boat like a leash.

Truebold smiled in understanding. "Never seen an efreet? They're used to pull ships across the sea. Sand's too thick for wind alone."

Jozlyn gasped. "That's cruel! It's chained up like a prisoner."

"*Heh-heh-hah-har-hargh*," Grinshine chuckled, and Truebold joined him.

"Efreet aren't prisoners, lass," the captain explained. "They aren't even alive. They're just air toughened up by magic." He wiggled his fingers. "Ye know, by the spell of a witch."

"Enchantress," Jozlyn corrected.

"Huh?" Truebold asked.

"A witch—oh, never mind." Jozlyn gave up in exasperation.

Josh jumped in to prevent an argument. "When do we leave?"

Scratching his bald head, Captain Truebold mumbled something then shrugged. "We can depart now, if yer ready."

We nodded eagerly. For the first time since arriving in Prospect Peak, I felt good about what was happening. If anyone could sail us to Silvermight, it was a crew of dwarves. Silvermight had been their home.

"All aboard!" Captain Truebold shouted.

29

Sailing is boring business, at least for passengers. Jozlyn, Josh, and I started our voyage to Silvermight by wandering the decks of the *Errant* but quickly ran out of room. There just weren't that many places to go on a ship.

For the most part, we tried to stay out of the dwarves' way. Captain Truebold and his busy crew scurried here and there, turning sails, tightening ropes, and studying charts. Sailing a ship looked very complicated, and we were glad just to watch.

Glad, but bored.

Endless sand surrounded us—white sand, gold sand, brown and silver. It splashed like sea spray and drifted in the air. Our clothes, hair, and places I'd rather not mention were covered with it. When I moved my jaw, my teeth made crunching noises.

"Is Silvermight an island?" Josh wondered as the three of

us sat on the deck with our feet dangling over the side.

"I don't know how it could be anything else," I said after a moment's thought.

The Sandy Sea was an empty desert. The only land we'd seen stabbed up through the sand like tiny mountain peaks. The mini-islands reminded me of the night we'd spent with Gramble in Croneswart Swamp.

"Silvermight isn't a place," Captain Truebold said from behind us, "not anymore. It vanished with the coming of the sand."

Jozlyn turned to peer up at him. "You mean it's buried?"

Truebold stared out at the sand with a distant look in his eyes before answering. "Nope, not buried. *Gone*. See that mountain over there?"

We looked to where he pointed at one of the many lumps that stuck up maybe thirty feet from the sand. There was nothing remarkable about it.

"Accordin' to our charts and history books," Truebold explained, "that mountain is the Clanhorn, a very special place to our people."

Josh shook his head. "It's just a pile of rocks."

A sad smile turned the captain's lips. "A mighty silver fortress once stood on that pile of rocks. Now nothin' remains. Not a single block."

Finally, we understood. Silvermight wasn't a secret island or a city hidden beneath the sand. It was a place that had disappeared without a trace.

"We've been lookin' to find lost Silvermight fer hundreds o' years," Truebold added without checking to see if we were still listening. His thoughts had taken him far away.

The four of us watched the horizon silently. The ship sailed on, the sand rolled and sprayed, and the scenery never changed.

My thoughts wandered a bit but always came back to the same question. If Silvermight didn't exist anymore, how were Captain Truebold and his crew taking us to it?

Josh broke my concentration with a tap to my arm.

"See that?" he asked, pointing into the sand.

I squinted down and shook my head. There was nothing to see but sand.

"There!" Jozlyn exclaimed, pointing in a new direction closer to the ship's hull.

Movement caught my eye, a red flash like blood. But nowhere near where Jozlyn and Josh pointed.

I gripped the rail in front of me and brought up my feet. "Something's down there," I hissed. Something alive and very big.

A blood red, shark-like fin broke the surface of the sand. But this fin had an eye in its center. A yellow, glassy fish eye.

Jozlyn shrieked as Josh yanked me back from the rail.

Clack!

An enormous pincer swiped by my face, snapping viciously. If Josh hadn't grabbed me, I'd have lost my head!

130

"Get down!" he shouted, and we threw ourselves to the deck but not before we saw what was out there.

Dozens of blood red bodies squirmed in the sand like giant worms. They snapped and screeched and—

Started to climb the sides of the ship!

Clack-clack. Clack!

30

"Lobsterpods!" a dwarven crewman shouted, charging forward with a bucket in his hands. With a roar, he heaved its contents over the rail onto the nearest creature.

The lobsterpod—that was the name of the red, clawed monster—squealed and tumbled into the sand, shrinking before our eyes.

"Water!" I cried, amazed and horrified at the same time. The lobsterpods shrank in water.

But in an ocean of sand, where could we find water?

Lobsterpods clawed up the hull and circled the ship like sharks in a feeding frenzy. It would take a rainstorm to drive them all away. In minutes they'd swarm the boat, and we'd be finished.

About twenty feet long, the lobsterpods resembled a weird cross between lobsters and sharks. Huge front claws and toothy mouths made perfect weapons. Jointed insect legs enabled them to climb almost any surface.

"Get back! Get back!" Captain Truebold bellowed.

I rolled over to see him and Grinshine riding a crazy-looking wagon pushed by a team of dwarves. Truebold clutched a wide hose sticking out from the wagon's front, and Grinshine pumped a metal lever attached to its back end.

The strange contraption reminded me of an elephant, and I almost expected water to squirt from the hose in Truebold's hands like a trunk.

G-g-g-g-gug! It rumbled over the deck. As it neared the rail, Captain Truebold raised the hose and took aim.

Gwoooosh!

Roaring funnels of water exploded from the hose, blasting into the lobsterpods. The monsters squealed and flailed their claws helplessly, shrinking and slipping off the ship.

A cheer erupted among the crew but was cut short as more lobsterpods scurried over the rail. Each time Truebold soaked one, another took its place. The army was endless!

"Left! To the left!" the captain shouted. "More pressure!" His face and bald head were flushed with strain.

Gwoooosh!

The dwarves heaved the wagon, and Grinshine furiously pumped the lever. Jets of water drenched the advancing lobsterpods, but more kept coming. The wagon was going to have to give up ground.

"Josh!" Jozlyn called. "Your sword!"

Josh scrambled to his feet and took off, and I followed. I didn't have a sword but running felt a lot better than lying on the deck like a possum.

We dodged puddles and shrunken, squirming lobsterpods. Their tiny claws snapped at us, and we kicked at them in disgust.

Even small, the creatures were nasty beasts!

"One!" I shouted as my boot connected and sent a mini-lobsterpod flying. "Two, three!" Two more flew after the first.

Josh caught on and started to count along with me. "Four and...five!" he added to our total.

The game was almost fun until a lobsterpod snagged the toe of my boot and refused to let go. I shook and shook my leg but the critter wouldn't budge.

"Take off your boot!" Jozlyn yelled. We'd managed to cross to her side of the deck.

"Take it—I don't have an extra!" I protested.

The trademark scowl shut me up quick. I ripped the boot from my foot and tossed it over the rail. "Six!" I counted, meaning the lobsterpod that went with my boot.

Jozlyn shook her head. "I didn't mean throw it over the side. You're such a *boy*!"

I wanted to scowl back at her, but she turned to Josh. Holding her miniature broom in hand, she raised her hands above his sword and chanted.

134

Day follows night.
Hot turns to cold.
Loose ties up tight.
Young becomes old.

The flames on Josh's sword began to flicker and flutter as if caught in the wind. Their dark blue color softened, becoming almost invisible.

Jozlyn continued to chant, shouting above the noise of battle. Then in a two-handed swing, she swatted the sword with her broom.

Wet dampens dry.
Flood drowns the spark.
Soak, do not fry,
Sand lobster-shark!

A roaring filled the air like when you hold a shell up to your ear. But this was a hundred times louder. It ended with a sharp slurping sound.

Vvvvrrrip!

Josh's sword turned into a wiggling wave, hissing like a serpent. Its fire disappeared, and a watery tentacle thrashed from its hilt like it was alive!

"Yes!" Josh cheered and tore off after the lobsterpods swarming the rail.

I turned to Jozlyn. "Me, too!" I begged, reaching for her arm. I wanted to help. To prove that I wasn't the baby of the quest.

As I reached for her, the *Errant* lurched sideways under the weight of the attacking lobsterpods. My bare foot slipped in a puddle, and I went sprawling.

THHUDD!

I tried to catch myself on a rail but hit my head and fell. Lying on the deck, I saw Josh lashing out with his water-sword. Lobsterpods surrounded him.

Then my world went black.

31

Err-rint. Err-rint.

When I came awake, I wished I hadn't. Pain drummed in my forehead, and I felt woozy like the world was tilting back and forth.

"*Whoaah!*" I gasped, throwing out my arms for balance. Doing so only made the world sway more.

Err-rint. Err-rint.

"Hey, easy! Relax!" Jozlyn chuckled softly. "You gave yourself quite a shiner."

We were in a cabin below deck. The swaying sensation was me rocking in a hammock to the roll of the sea.

"The lobsterpods—what happened?" I asked as I gingerly prodded the welt around my right eye. It was really sore!

"They're gone," Jozlyn smiled from a hammock across the cabin. "We shrank enough of them to scare the rest off."

That was good news, but I still couldn't help feeling sorry for myself. Like always, I hadn't done a thing to help. Josh and Jozlyn had rescued me.

Some leader! I sulked, feeling ashamed. *What would happen if Jozlyn and Josh had to depend on me?*

"Up for taking a walk?" Jozlyn asked. "There's something we've been waiting to show you."

I struggled out of the hammock without a word. Knowing that everyone had been forced to wait for me didn't put me in a talkative mood.

Jozlyn lead us out of the cabin and back above deck. The sun had nearly set, and the sky was darkening. I'd been unconscious for hours!

Josh met us right away. "Hi, sleepyhead," he grinned.

I grunted in response. I'd knocked myself out during a battle and he called me *sleepyhead*? No one thought I was much of a leader.

Josh shrugged. "Well, Jasiah, we made it. We're at Silvermight."

My jaw dropped and I forgot all about feeling sorry for myself. "What? Where?" I asked, spinning around excitedly.

The scenery hadn't changed. The Sandy Sea stretched to the horizon in every direction. It was hard to tell where the sand ended and the sky began.

"There," Captain Truebold pointed. He and Grinshine leaned against the rail not far away. "But we ain't goin' no closer."

Grinshine snickered in agreement. "*Heh-heh-hah-har-hargh.*"

The captain pointed at a curious mound rising from the sand. At first I thought it was another rocky island but it was too smooth. And too shiny.

It almost looked like silver....

"The guardian to our old home," Truebold explained. "A-hundred foot statue of solid silver. It's all that's left, and it won't let anyone pass. Not without the password, but we can't remember it."

The mound sure didn't look one hundred feet tall. Maybe ten. It rose up like a half- scoop of ice cream. Two pointy arms stuck out from its sides.

"A helmet?" I guessed.

"Aye, that it is," Truebold said. "But get any closer and the statue'll stand up outta the sand. Then ye'll see its real size."

Captain Truebold was trying to persuade us to leave the statue alone. He didn't want anything to do with it.

But we'd come too far to turn back. The second piece of the Dragonsbane Horn was close. We had to investigate.

I turned to face the captain. "Can we borrow a row-boat?" I asked then glanced at my one bare foot. "And a pair of boots?"

The dwarf tugged on his beard-braids, and for once Grinshine didn't chuckle. "I was afraid ye'd ask that,"

Truebold admitted with a sigh.

He and Grinshine turned to the rail and looked down. There in the sand floated a small rowboat tied to the *Errant*. It wasn't much of a boat, but it had two oars and a pair of new boots sitting on a seat.

"Better go 'fore it gets too dark," Truebold said without looking at us. His avoidance gave me the feeling that he didn't plan on seeing us again.

A rope ladder led down to the rowboat. I went first, put on the boots, and grabbed the oars. Since I wouldn't be much help in a fight, I decided I might as well row.

Josh and Jozlyn sat together in the front, but I couldn't see them because I had to sit backward. That's the way rowing works. But I heard Josh draw his sword.

"I think you should show it the Horn," he suggested to me. By *it*, he meant the statue. "Maybe it'll think we're friends."

"*Ungh*," I grunted. Rowing in sand was tough! The sea might act and look watery but it felt like molasses. My arms burned with strain.

C-R-E-E-E-C-H!

A horrible grinding noise caused me to throw down the oars and cover my ears. Sudden waves rocked the rowboat.

"The Horn!" Josh cried. "Show it the Horn!"

I spun in my seat, fumbling for the Horn. The waves made it almost impossible to keep my balance, and sand poured into the boat.

140

C-R-E-E-E-C-H!

Grinding like rusty gears, the silver statue heaved itself out of the sand. A huge shadow fell over our boat.

"*INTRUDERS!*" the statue boomed in an awful voice that sounded like a clap of thunder right over our heads.

Just like Captain Truebold had said, the statue was at least one hundred feet tall and made of solid silver. It looked like a gigantic dwarf dressed for war. Clutched in its shining silver hands was a double-headed battle hammer.

My hands shook as I frantically waved the Horn over my head. "We have the Dragonsbane Horn! Don't attack!"

With a screech of metal, the statue swung its massive head. Glowing silver eyes fixed on me.

"*INTRUDER!*" it bellowed again and raised its mighty hammer to attack.

Try to Swim! Outlook's Grim!

32

"Look out!" I screamed, getting a mouthful of sand.

Showing the Horn to the statue wasn't working. The guardian either didn't recognize it or didn't care. We needed to escape, not make friends.

C-R-E-E-E-C-H!

The statue raised its arms behind its head, metal grinding. Its great hammer took aim on our tiny rowboat.

"Jump!" we all cried at the same time. There was no way our boat could survive a blow from a weapon that size.

The statue attacked as we leaped. Josh and Jozlyn plunged over the sides, and I dove off the back end. The hammer connected a heartbeat behind.

THWONCH!

The blast sent me tumbling through the sand. Broken bits of wood pelted me. Waves crashed over my head, dragging me down.

"Help!" I coughed, clawing my way to the surface. Swimming in the Sandy Sea was like trying to run through snow buried up to my neck.

The force of the hammer's blast had set off an earthquake in the sand. Or was it a *sand*quake? A *sea*quake?

Crazy thoughts filled my head. Things I shouldn't have been thinking. I saw Uncle Arick battling the shaddim, Josh floating like a balloon, and Medium Mirelda's spinning globe.

Even the words to the pirates' song echoed hauntingly in my ears.

Try to swim!
Outlook's grim.
You can't swim.

The song was right. I couldn't swim. I was going to drown!

Thap!

Something struck the back of my head. Not sand or debris from the boat. Something solid and with a certain swampy odor....

Thap! It came again, urgently.

"Grab on!" Josh yelled.

Struggling hard in the sloshing sand, I couldn't believe what I saw. It was crazier than my crazy thoughts.

Josh dangled in the air, hanging from a long silver chain. His legs kicked as he twirled awkwardly. Above him, the

144

airy efreet from Captain Truebold's ship floated in place like a hummingbird.

We were saved! The dwarves had sent the efreet to drag us out of the sand. I could have cheered if it wouldn't have earned me another mouthful of sand.

Josh's boot reared back for a third kick.

"I see you!" I gasped, trying to let him know before he whacked me again.

Thap! Lucky me. His smelly boot thumped me square on the nose.

"No, I *smell* you!" I corrected, my voice squeaking and eyes watering. "Jozlyn was right. You need a bath!"

Josh flailed his foot. "Just grab on! The statue's getting tired of smashing up the boat."

One glance toward the statue and what was left of our boat told me he was right. The rowboat was demolished. Broken planks bobbed in the sand.

C-R-E-E-E-C-H!

The statue raised its hammer and turned to us.

"*INTRUDERS!*" it roared.

Boy, was I getting tired of hearing that.

"Hurry!" Josh cried.

I didn't comment on the swampy smell this time. I wrapped my arms around his boot and closed my eyes.

Throush! Throush!

The statue charged after us, kicking up tidal waves of sand.

"Get us away from here!" Josh ordered the efreet as soon as I had a good grip on his boot.

We shot upward immediately. My elbows snapped straight, and I lost my stomach. Wind blew sand into my face.

Throush! Throush!

The statue wasn't giving up, but it couldn't match the speed of the magical efreet. In seconds we were out of range, spinning slowly in the air like a yo-yo on the end of its string.

I opened my eyes to look down and my stomach rolled. We were a lot higher than I'd expected! The statue and the *Errant* were far below. They looked tiny, like toys.

"Don't let go!" I told Josh between clenched teeth. Falling into the sand at this height wouldn't be anything like diving over the side of the rowboat.

"No duh!" he shot back. Of course he wouldn't let go. Not on purpose anyway.

Except for the height, I was starting to feel pretty good about our escape. The run-in with the silver guardian could have gone worse. The three of us could—

The three of us?

My head shot up in alarm. Josh dangled from the efreet, and I dangled from Josh.

But where was Jozlyn?

I searched the sand but found no sign of her.

Cradled to Grave

33

"Josh!" I cried. "Where's Jozlyn?"

He mumbled something like *cheese in eye*, but I couldn't be sure. He had his teeth gritted against the sand, and wind whistled loudly in my ears.

"Stop! We have to find her. Turn around!" How could he leave his sister buried in the sand?

Josh scowled at me, his teeth still clenched. "She's— in—my—pocket," he growled slowly.

I blinked. "What?" *She's in my* only sounded a little bit like *cheese in eye*, but neither made sense.

Josh's face turned red with frustration, and I cringed. I didn't need him mad at me. His boot was the only thing keeping me in the air.

"Dreamsafe Den," he explained. "Remember the flowers? Jozlyn shrank herself." He got a mouthful of sand for his trouble.

The magic shrinking flowers! Jozlyn really was in his pocket!

To prove it, her squeaky, shrunken voice piped up. It sounded like a chipmunk imitating her. "I'm safe! A good witch is always prepared."

"Good *enchantress*!" I shouted back automatically.

"Whatever!" Jozlyn squeaked in a huff.

Knowing that all three of us were safe, I felt better for real. Well, better except for the height and the fact that my arms were starting to hurt. I hoped we reached the *Errant* soon.

But when I looked for the ship, it wasn't there. Neither was the statue.

I kicked my legs, trying to spin myself around. Where were we going? The efreet was taking us in the wrong direction.

"Stop wiggling!" Josh grumbled. "You're going to knock us into the sand."

"But the ship!" I wailed. "I can't see it."

"I know," he replied. "I told the efreet to get us out of there. It must think I meant away from the statue *and* the ship."

"Well, tell it to turn around!" I demanded.

Josh shook his foot in annoyance, but not hard enough to shake me loose. "Don't you think I tried that?"

I bit my tongue and changed the subject. "Can you ask it to fly faster then? My arms are getting tired."

That was an understatement. Sweat covered my hands, and my arms shook with fatigue. My fingers felt so stiff I feared I'd never be able to straighten them.

"How do you think I feel—*oh*!" Josh started but halted with a sudden gasp.

The efreet wrapped a bulging arm around his waist and hauled him up. It cradled him like a sack of groceries. With its other arm, the efreet scooped me into a similar position.

Josh's face was only inches from mine and he smirked. "There, that better?"

I grunted. "Like you had anything to do with it." Still, being carried was a lot better than hanging onto Josh's smelly boot.

How long we flew, I couldn't say. I think I even slept on and off. But every time I opened my eyes, the scenery was the same. Dark sand below us, starry night sky above.

Maybe we'll never land, I thought dreamily. *Maybe we'll…*.

Light stung my eyes. It was dawn! I'd really fallen asleep that time. Silvery sand sparkled as far as I could see.

There was something else ahead, too. Something large and made of wood sticking out of the sand.

A ship! Maybe it was the *Errant*.

"Josh, wake up," I prodded. "I think we're almost there." Not that I knew where *there* was.

He mumbled something and squinted. "I don't see

anything."

I'd forgotten again that he couldn't see as far as me.

"It looks like a ship…" I started to explain then changed my mind as we got closer. "No, a whole bunch of ships."

I gasped as the sight became more clear. Dozens of ships bobbed and lurched in the sand. Most were partially buried, some with only their masts poking above the surface like skeletal fingers clawing out of the grave.

The ships scraped against rocks and bumped into one another with the rhythm of the surf. Their tattered sails fluttered weakly. Their splintered hulls gaped like fresh wounds.

"It's a graveyard," Josh whispered.

The efreet flew straight into the tangle of ships. Whenever the shadow of a rotting sail or cracked mast touched me, I felt an unpleasant chill crawl across my skin.

At last we came to a stop aboard a small ship. The efreet set us on the vessel's warped deck and turned its blank face to us.

"*Grrreeedhauuunt Ssshallowsss*," it hissed like an icy wind. "*Farrr awaaay*."

Then it glided silently back to sea, leaving us in the ruin of dead ships.

Greedhaunt Shallows

34

Once the efreet had gone, Josh and I slumped to the deck with our heads down. We'd reached a new low, and our quest seemed hopeless.

All around, abandoned ships creaked like unhappy spirits. The noise echoed throughout Greedhaunt Shallows, filling the air with eerie music.

"Now what?" Josh muttered, not really expecting me to answer.

I shook my head without looking at him. I didn't know. I'd thought we would find the second piece of the Horn at Silvermight. I'd thought we'd be on our way home.

But I'd thought a lot of things wrong.

We'd failed at Silvermight. We'd lost the dwarves. And we had less hope of finding the Horn than ever.

Where were we supposed to look for it without any clues? The Sandy Sea was huge!

"Help me out," Jozlyn's tiny voice chirped.

Josh pulled her from his pocket, and she used her magic flower to return to normal size. Then she stood with her hands on her hips and scowled at us. She'd never looked more like a big sister.

"So that's it?" she challenged. "You've given up?"

Josh waved an arm to indicate our bleak surroundings. "Look at this place. What are we supposed to do?"

I agreed with him, but I'd never have said it like that. Not out loud or to Jozlyn.

"What are we…what…?" Jozlyn sputtered, throwing up her arms. "We're supposed to find the Dragonsbane Horn. Some deputy you are, just giving up."

That did it. Josh jumped to his feet and pointed angrily at her. "I'll bet you think being a *witch* is so much better. Why don't you use some of your magic to find the Horn." He purposefully used *witch* instead of *enchantress*.

From there, the conversation got worse. Being brother and sister, they really knew how to get under each other's skin.

I decided it was time to take another walk. Exploring the creepy ships seemed like more fun than listening.

Of course I didn't mean to go far. It just happened. I was just trying to get away for awhile.

The marooned ships were packed so closely together that I could step, climb, or jump from one to another. I tiptoed across gangplanks, shimmied along fallen masts, and swung

152

from ropes like a swashbuckler.

For a bit, I forgot where I was and why I was there. Thoughts of the Horn and our quest vanished from my mind. I just had fun exploring.

When I noticed the sun overhead, I realized that I was completely lost. Hours had passed since I'd left Jozlyn and Josh.

I cupped my hands around my mouth and called out to them. "Josh! Jozlyn!" There was no answer, so I tried again. And again and again.

The sound of my voice echoed across Greedhaunt Shallows. Unseen things creaked and groaned in response, but nothing friendly made a sound.

I was alone.

What were you thinking! I scolded myself. *What a stupid thing to do!*

My breathing quickened and my heart started to race. I was lost in a graveyard!

Chilling questions nagged me. Why were so many ships here? Because of monsters or a magical curse? Where had all the sailors gone?

I heard sounds that weren't there. Or were they? I saw things in the corner of my eye that vanished when I turned my head.

Blindly, I started to run. I felt eyes all over me, watching me. Eyes filled with anger and greed. Eyes of the dead.

My foot came down on nothing, a jagged hole in the

deck. I threw out my arms and tumbled into darkness.

"*Ungh!*" I grunted, landing on a heap of sacks that squished unpleasantly beneath my weight. From my back, I could see up through the hole in the ceiling.

I needed to catch my breath. To calm—

Eet-eet.

Something moved in the darkness across the cabin. Not the wind ruffling a sail or boards creaking in the sand.

Something alive.

I rolled into a crouch, the sacks bursting and oozing with sticky wetness beneath me. They stank of garbage, and I guessed they had been stuffed with food for the ship's missing sailors.

Two small lights blinked at me from the darkness. They were eyes—*rat eyes!* I knew without doubt. I wasn't alone after all.

Eet-eet, the rat squeaked. Then it started to waddle toward me with a noticeable limp.

I watched curiously as it approached. Rats were nasty creatures but not all that dangerous. I could probably scare this one away or outrun it. The poor thing was limping badly.

It hobbled into the light coming from the hole, and my blood went cold.

Instead of four legs, the rat had three, and one of them was a tiny peg leg of solid gold. Its mangy fur drooped in wet strands like blackened banana peels. A jeweled stickpin stuck up where its tails should be.

The rat wasn't alive! But it wasn't quite dead either. It was somewhere in between, and I suddenly had doubts about my being able to scare it.

I decided to run instead, only there was nowhere to go. I was trapped in the bottom of the ship.

Eet-eet, chattered the rat-thing.

35

Without taking my eyes from the ghastly rat, I scooted cautiously down the pile of sacks. They burst beneath my feet like rotten fruit, soaking into my boots.

Blurk! Splock!

Split open, their stench was horrible. My eyes watered, and my stomach gurgled. Even the rat twitched its nose in seeming discomfort.

"Pretty bad, huh?" I said to it, not knowing why. Maybe I hoped I'd sound confident or threatening. Maybe I was scared.

It's only a rat, I tried to convince myself. *Just a three-legged rat. What would Josh or Jozlyn do?*

I didn't wonder about the answer long. Josh and Jozlyn were brave. They were heroes. They would fight.

I stopped thinking and charged.

The rat jerked anxiously when it saw me coming, its legs

spread like a spider's. Its pointy jaw opened, and diamond fangs flashed in its mouth.

What had turned the rat into such a gruesome mismatch? It was half-animal and half-confusion, like a puzzle forced together with all the wrong pieces.

Clah-krattle!

My boot didn't wonder as it drew back, kicked, and hit home. It struck the rat, and the creature collapsed like a bundle of sticks. Bones and sparkling trinkets clattering onto the floor.

Just like that, it was over. I'd defeated the rat, or whatever it was, and I let out a sigh. I'd finally done something heroic.

I might have felt better about it if I hadn't been screaming the whole time.

Crates and metal chests cluttered the area, not just the pile of sacks. There was no sense or order to their placement. They looked as if the shop had been turned upside down, shaken, and then dropped into the sand.

One of the chests was open, and a gleam caught my eye. So did the glimpse of a door I hadn't noticed.

Jewels! The chest was full of jewels. Enough to satisfy the greediest pirate. Rubies, emeralds, and sapphires twinkled faintly from beneath a layer of dust.

I forgot about seeing the door and reached out my hand. I was rich.

Take yer fill an' more, a breathy voice hissed into my ear.

It had the sound of a serpent. *Take it with the blessin' o' Cap'n Halfhand*.

I pulled my hand away and spun around. "Who…?" I gasped in alarm but saw no one.

The voice chuckled dryly, still right in my ear. *Go ahead, laddie. Ye know ye wanna*.

I flailed my arms about my head like a swarm of bees was attacking. "Where are you?" I demanded.

Take 'em now. Might as well. The greed'll get ye 'fore long. The voice chuckled again.

"No!" I shouted, throwing my hands over my ears. When I could still hear the laughter, I started to babble without words. Anything to drown out the haunting sound.

My thoughts cleared immediately. What did I want with a pirate's treasure? Look at the good it had done him….

That's it, I realized suddenly. *The mystery of Greedhaunt Shallows*. The ships were trapped because of the greed of their crews. It lured them with promises of wealth then never let them escape.

I ran from the cabin and slammed the door behind me.

A ladder-like flight of stairs led up to the main deck. In the warmth of the sun, I forgot about my chilling encounter with Captain Halfhand and remembered that I hadn't seen Josh or Jozlyn in hours.

Like before, I cupped my hands and called to them. I faced every direction, stood on crates, leaned from the rail, and yelled until my voice was hoarse.

Nothing worked. Josh and Jozlyn were too far away. I needed something to make me louder. Something like a trumpet or a....

I froze in mid-shout, my hands dropping to my sides. I did have something loud. Something Jozlyn and Josh would be sure to hear.

I had the Dragonsbane Horn.

36

Did I dare blow the Horn? What would happen? The last thing I needed was a flight of dragons swooping down on me, breathing fire and ice. I was in enough trouble.

I sat on a crate and rolled the Horn between my palms. It wasn't the *real* Dragonsbane Horn. Just a part of it. Blowing it would probably just make noise.

Which was exactly what I needed.

That decided it. I stood on the crate and brought the Horn to my lips. "Here goes," I whispered then puffed out my cheeks.

I'd pushed the air out of my lungs before when blowing on birthday cakes and dandelion seeds. This was nothing like that. The Horn sucked my breath out like it wanted to be blown. Like it was eager to be heard and to work its magic.

I thought it would never stop.

Soft at first, its sound rose like a charging stampede. It rumbled, it shrieked, it howled and blared. It boomed noisily and sang of forgotten things far away.

In its song, I heard the clash of swords, the ringing of hammers, and the chanting of wizards' spells. I felt old and wise, a part of everything everywhere.

I felt whole.

I lowered the Horn and shouted triumphantly into the sky. "I am Jasiah Dragonsbane!"

Never before had I truly known who I was. Never had I guessed the part I'd play on our quest.

But I knew now, and I trembled with fear and responsibility. *I* was the Dragonsbane. *I* was the Horn. The quest was about me just like Uncle Arick had said.

In fact, there was no quest without me. Only I could summon the Horn's magic. Like a king's crown passed from father to son, the power of the Dragonsbane Horn had been given to me.

My body went numb with shock, and I collapsed onto the deck. The knowledge of the Horn was too much to take. I was just a kid. Someone should have warned me.

Seconds or hours passed. I couldn't tell how long and didn't care. There was so much to think about. So much to fear. I needed time to recover.

Skrawt!

A piercing squawk made me cringe. Far above, something circled the sky, descending rapidly.

As it came closer, I made out wings, sharp talons, gleaming scales, and a tail that lashed back and forth like a snake.

I recognized the creature instantly.

A dragon had come for the Horn.

Talon Wyvern

37

Seeing the dragon coming, I thought two things. The first was "Help!" The second was, "That's a pretty small dragon."

As it approached, it never seemed to get bigger. At least not *big* like I thought a dragon should be.

Luckily, it didn't breath fire or shoot lightning from its eyes. In fact, it didn't do anything hostile. It just squawked and circled lower.

Skrawt!

Not even its squawk was threatening. The sound reminded me of a greeting, not a battle cry. It was like the creature was saying *hello*.

So I took a chance. I raised my arm and waved.

Skrawk!

— You wear the gauntlet. —

"*Wha*—?" I gasped, falling onto my rump. The creature

had spoken! I'd heard its words in my mind and under-stood them like I could speak dragon.

"What are you?" I asked out loud.

The creature arched its wings and landed on a nearby crate, giving me my first good look at it. I realized some-thing important right away.

The creature wasn't a dragon.

It reminded me of a cross between a lizard and a bird of prey—an eagle or falcon. It had a dragon's shape but wasn't much larger than a crow, except for its long tail and longer neck. Feathers and scales of blue, purple, and red intertwined to form tough armor over its body. Silvery wings like liquid metal took the place of front arms.

It was beautiful and dangerous, but its eyes amazed me most. They peered at me with surprising intelligence.

This was no ordinary bird-lizard! Not that bird-lizards were ever ordinary, but—

Skrawt!

The creature squawked again, and words and images filled my mind. It was talking to me!

—I am a wyvern, a relative of the dragon. I am called Talon in your language. You could not pronounce my real name.—

A series of squawks, whistles, and hisses echoed confus-ingly in my head. Sounds I'd never be able to repeat or remember. They were Talon's real name.

The wyvern continued.

—You are the Dragonsbane. You wear the gauntlet and protect the Horn. I am the Companion. I protect the Dragonsbane.—

It took a minute for that to sink in.

—I protect you.— Talon clarified as I pondered.

"Like a pet? A talking pet?" I blurted excitedly. "Wait until Josh and Jozlyn—"

—No.— Talon interjected, the feathers on her neck ruffling like the fur on a cat's back. —I am the Companion. Your equal. Perhaps one day your friend.—

Feeling sheepish, I mumbled an apology. "*I*-I'm sorry." What a way to introduce myself! *Hi, I'm Jasiah, a complete buffoon. Will you be my friend?*

—Apology accepted. You are young. There is time enough to train you, *buffoon*.—

A sparkle of mischief played in Talon's intelligent eyes. *Buffoon?* She'd read my thoughts and was making fun of me!

I fired back at her. "Alright, *birdbrain*, where do we go from here? I need to find my friends."

Talon squawked and hissed softly, the wyvern way of laughing. Then she spread her gleaming wings and took to the air.

—Close your eyes and think of me. We will find them.—

Suspiciously, I did as she asked, and the ship lurched dizzily beneath me. Wind howled in my ears and I felt light-headed. Below me, I spotted a small boy sitting with

165

his eyes closed. He looked so familiar….

The boy was me!

I cried out, my eyes opening and arms windmilling for balance. I felt like I was falling and going to be sick.

How could I be in the air with Talon and on the deck at the same time?

From above, Talon hissed a chuckle. —You are safe. Fear not. Let my eyes guide yours.—

My head shot up, and I spotted her slowly circling the ship. Had I been seeing what she saw from up there?

Let my eyes guide yours.

Talon sent her thoughts down. —Now you understand. Try again.—

That was it! I'd been seeing what she saw. When I closed my eyes and concentrated, I could see though her eyes.

I took a deep breath, nodded, and closed my eyes. This time I didn't panic when I felt myself racing upward. The feeling was an illusion. My body never left the deck.

Once I got used to it, seeing through Talon's eyes was incredible. I flew with her, and she put on a show. We looped in great circles, streaked the air in breathtaking dives, and skimmed the sand of the sea like a crane gliding over a pond.

I never wanted to land! Through Talon's eyes, I could fly anywhere.

—Your friends.— the wyvern reminded, and I sighed.

166

We needed to find Josh and Jozlyn, but I hated to end our thrilling flight.

"You're right," I agreed. "Let's hurry!"

Talon sped off, winging high over Greedhaunt Shallows. The rotting ships blurred beneath her, but her sharp eyes didn't miss a thing. Mine didn't either because I saw through hers.

Greedhaunt Shallows occupied a larger area than I'd realized. There must have been over one hundred ships caught in its sandy clutches.

When movement caught Talon's attention, she dropped in for a closer look. The sudden descent tickled my stomach, but I managed to keep my eyes closed.

What a strange thing to do! Keep my eyes closed in order to see.

Talon swooped below a tangle of sails, and a small group of men came into view. They stood in a circle, clutching strange, oversized weapons in their hands. One looked to be holding the oar from a boat.

Pirates! I recognized. The men were too tall to be dwarves and too thin for honest work. They were almost as skinny as skeletons.

Trapped in the center of their ring, Jozlyn and Josh huddled closely together.

"Talon, come back!" I cried, not knowing if she'd hear my voice or sense my thoughts. So long as she returned, it didn't matter.

I needed her near so that she could lead me across Greedhaunt Shallows. Jozlyn and Josh had been captured by pirates!

38

Talon returned almost immediately. Not much moves faster than a flying wyvern.

— Hold out your arm — she told me.

Confused, I did. My left arm.

— Your other arm, *humanbrain*. The one wearing the gauntlet. —

"Oh, so that's…" I mumbled, putting the pieces together. The gauntlet was for Talon. Uncle Arick had given it to me, knowing I'd eventually meet the wyvern.

That was one more mystery solved, thanks to the Horn.

Talon swooped down and landed on my outstretched arm. The gauntlet protected me from her sharp claws.

— See that, you *can* be trained. — Her eyes sparkled playfully again.

"Who landed on *my* arm, lizard-beak?" I countered. "Looks like I've got you trained." I liked Talon. She was smart and fun, like an adult who hadn't forgotten what it's like to be a kid.

— We will see about that. Later. For now, let's rescue your friends. —

That was like an adult, too. Talon knew when to play and when to get to business. She never mixed them up by doing the wrong thing at the wrong time.

We started after the pirates. Talon zipped from rail to mast and from crate to crow's nest, always one step ahead of me. Or was that one *flap* ahead? When I caught her, she darted to her next perch.

I was breathing hard and sweating when we scampered onto the forecastle of a sagging ship. That's the front most deck where the wheel is. A forecastle is raised above the other decks so the captain can see everything that goes on.

I crouched behind a row of barrels and peered down at the pirates. Talon perched on my arm, her dragon's tail lashing anxiously.

The first thing I noticed was that the pirates weren't exactly pirates. They were skeletons and half-men.

Yellowed bones peeked from beneath their tattered clothing. Rusty chains and oars dangled from their shoulders. Gems glinted in their eye sockets. Scraps of metal and bits of jewelry held them together like buckles.

Ghouls of Greedhaunt Shallows, I decided. The pirates weren't human anymore. Their greed and this place had turned them into monsters.

One of the pirates gestured at Jozlyn and Josh with a short, silver rod. He gripped it awkwardly in his skeletal hand because his first two fingers and thumb were missing.

He was Captain Halfhand! The pirate who'd tried to tempt me with cursed jewels.

The captain cackled and shoved Josh in the back, pushing him and Jozlyn onto a gangplank. "Into the sand with ye!" he shouted gleefully. In the sea below, a lobsterpod circled hungrily.

"We need a distraction," I whispered to Talon. "Fast!"

She nodded and leaped into the air with a screech, not her normal squawk. It was a threatening sound, and I thought I spotted smoke steaming from her mouth.

Can wyverns breathe fire? I wondered briefly.

Talon raced straight toward Captain Halfhand. Pirates lashed at her with their oars and chains. Those with hands swung bejeweled swords. She dodged them easily.

"Kill that bird!" Captain Halfhand shrieked. "It's after our loot." He frantically waved his silver rod like a general commanding troops.

In his two-fingered grip, the rod was an easy mark. Talon swooped in, stretched out her legs, and snatched it from the pirate.

The captain went berserk, howling and stomping. Clumps of rotting material fell from his body and clothes. "Not my Eye! Bring back my Eye, you scurvy bird!"

Listening to him, a memory tickled my mind. I'd heard

about an eye recently. A pirate's eye....

Talon soared over the rail then spun about in mid-air to face the raging captain and his monstrous crew. In one claw, she dangled Halfhand's precious rod dangerously over the sand.

I knew what she was thinking. She was trying to trade Josh and Jozlyn for the rod.

But the rod was too important to give up. I knew that but not exactly why. I couldn't let Talon drop it into the sea.

"No, Talon!" I yelled, giving myself away in the process. "Don't drop it!"

The pirates turned to me, startled to see someone else. So did Jozlyn and Josh.

"Jasiah!" they cried, then Jozlyn added, "We're coming!" She tore the miniature broom from her satchel and spread her arms.

"Oh, no, ye don't, missy," Captain Halfhand roared. He raised a slender arm fashioned from a gold-plated walking cane. Its polished handle served as his hand.

No wonder he'd held the Eye in his clumsy half hand. The cane didn't have fingers.

"Get the other whelp!" he ordered his crew. "The bird'll hafta come back then."

The ghoulish crew scowled at me and started to lumber toward the forecastle. Metal screeched and wood creaked as they marched.

I needed a weapon, but all I had was the Horn, and I

wasn't about to show that to the greedy pirates. They'd want it for themselves.

Luckily, Josh had his sword. Blue flames erupted as he drew it and lunged at Captain Halfhand before the pirate could strike.

Thwoffff!

The fiery blade slashed clean through Captain Halfhand's cane arm, and the pirate staggered back, surprised but not injured. The cane wasn't a real arm. It was just wood and gold plating.

The pause gave Jozlyn the time she needed. She chanted words that echoed across Greedhaunt Shallows.

Smile at me, enemy,
Bark worse than you bite.
Show this sea charity.
Find friends, not a fight.

Captain Halfhand heard her words and screamed in fury, charging forward. He lowered his bony shoulders and stomped onto the gangplank.

This time, Josh and Jozlyn didn't let the pirate get close. They shared a quick look then jumped.

"*Nooo!*" I wailed, but it was too late. They splashed into the sand and were gone.

"Let's get 'em, mates," a pirate growled.

I turned to see the crew as they climbed the stairs to the forecastle. They were almost on top of me.

"Talon!" I screamed. I was trapped and alone on a ship full of ghouls.

39

Greedhaunt pirates clattered up the stairs. They moved awkwardly, their skeletal bodies stiff and slow. Nothing about them was human but their shape.

Dull gemstones glinted from their hollow skulls. Tarnished jewelry dangled from their bony fingers and necks. Torn silk robes hung limply from their shoulders.

The pirates had given their health and their lives to greed.

I turned away, disgusted and afraid. Captain Halfhand had almost lured me with his false promises once. I couldn't let myself be taken!

But there was nowhere to go. I ran to the edge of the ship and turned my back to the rail. How I wished I could fly like an efreet!

The undead pirates stumbled closer. They raised weapons, canes, scepters, and oars. Their boots and golden peg legs scraped noisily on the deck.

"One last chance, boy," Captain Halfhand snarled as he pushed through the ranks of his ghoulish crew. "Call down yer bird."

I tried to respond, but my voice caught in my throat. I couldn't talk to him. He was a ghoul, a monster. Nothing but a squeaky noise passed my lips.

Laughter broke out among the crew. They clacked their jaws and stomped their weapons on the deck.

"Silence!" the captain roared without taking his eyes from me. "I need me Eye, boy. It ain't worth dyin' over, is it?"

I doubted it, but a memory still nagged me. What was so important about a pirate's eye?

The captain pointed his cane arm at my chest. The sliced end was jagged and sharp. "I'll count to three. One...."

He never finished.

Screeching, Talon streaked from the sky. She shot between us in a flash, shining like a piece of metal reflecting the sun.

"*Argh!*" Captain Halfhand grunted, throwing his arms up to protect his head. "Get it!"

For one brief moment, I saw Talon lunging at the pirate with her claws extended, then she became a speeding blur of color. A single word echoed in my mind.

—Jump!—

I didn't wait for her to tell me again. I twisted around, grasped the ship's rail, and vaulted over the edge.

Shhlooop!

The Sandy Sea swallowed me in a suffocating cocoon. Immense weight pinned my arms and legs. Darkness surrounded me.

I was sinking like a stone! I'd escaped the pirates only to drown.

"Talon!" I tried to shriek, but sand poured into my mouth. The darkness was thickening, becoming solid. I couldn't breathe….

Pain scalded the top of my head, and I was jerked upward. I tried to kick my legs but the sand was too thick.

Then suddenly there was light and air. My lungs heaved, and I pulled my arms up high enough to keep myself afloat.

Talon's voice chuckled in my mind. —I protect the Dragonsbane. Even if the clumsy buffoon cannot swim.—

The wyvern hovered above me, shaking sand out of her feathers. Her dragon's face looked to be smirking.

Seeing her, I realized what had happened. She'd dragged me out of the sand by the hair on my head. No wonder I'd felt such pain!

Instead of thanking her, I shouted childishly. "I'd better not be bald!"

Talon squinted at me with a motherly look. The kind you get when you stick your elbow in mashed potatoes while wearing your best outfit. —Turn around.—

Deciding I'd better keep quiet, I circled until the pirate ship came into view. Captain Halfhand and his crew scowled down at me, shaking their fists and whatever else they had for hands.

I gasped, paddling backwards. The pirates could easily hit me if they decided to start throwing things.

—Ignore them. Keep turning— Talon said.

It took all of my willpower not to swim away. I wanted to trust Talon, but I also wanted as much distance as possible between me and the pirates.

As I continued to turn, something flashed in the corner of my eye. Something very large and the color of dried blood.

At first I thought the pirates were throwing things. I imagined spears, anchors, buckets, and fishing nets splashing into the sand.

But none of those was red or nearly as dangerous as what was headed straight toward me.

I spotted a single bloated eye.

It belonged to a lobsterpod.

40

A lobsterpod! That was worse than Captain Halfhand and his pirates. Why had Talon betrayed me?

I flopped in a half-circle, splashing and kicking frantically. Swimming in the Sandy Sea was a challenge. Swimming fast was impossible.

"Why?" I cried between screams.

Talon didn't answer. Instead, two hands clutched the back of my tunic and hauled me out of the sand.

What? Lobsterpods didn't have hands.

I twisted around, trying to see behind me. Glimpses of the lobsterpod's armor-like shell spun dizzily in my vision. So did a patch of blonde hair.

"Jozlyn?" I gasped, disbelieving.

"Get on!" she shouted.

"And quit wiggling," Josh added, panting heavily.

Stunned, I quit moving. Josh and Jozlyn were riding the

lobsterpod!

Josh dragged me onto the creature's back, and I scrambled into a sitting position. I sat between my friends with Jozlyn in front. She gripped the lobsterpod's eye-fin like it was a horse's mane.

"Why isn't this thing attacking us?" I asked nervously.

Jozlyn beamed a smile over her shoulder. "Magic, silly! I made friends with Rusty before we jumped off the gangplank."

I blinked and Jozlyn giggled. "Rusty?" I asked.

Josh groaned. "She already named it," he said.

That reminded me of Talon. I'd made a new friend, too.

I looked into the sky and spotted the wyvern overhead. "That's Talon," I said. "She's a wyvern. She came when I blew the Horn. That's what this gauntlet—"

"Yep, we know," Jozlyn interjected. "We met her when you were playing with the pirates. She gave us this."

Jozlyn pushed Captain Halfhand's silver rod into my hands. Only now that I could see it up close, I saw that it wasn't a plain rod. It had round pieces of glass at both ends and five sections that narrowed toward its tip.

A spyglass! That's why Captain Halfhand had called it his Eye. With it, he could see faraway objects as if they were much closer.

Suddenly, some of the words to Medium Mirelda's fortune repeated in my head.

Set prow to ply
For pirate's eye
'Tween main and mountain peak.

That was it! Where I'd heard about a pirate's eye. Now if I could figure out why the spyglass was important….

"We thought of that, too," Josh said, and I realized I'd recited the fortune aloud.

"So we were supposed to find the spyglass?" I wondered, staring at the designs etched on its barrel. They were worn but I could still make out sailing ships, treasure chests, and—

The Dragonsbane Horn! A picture of the Horn was engraved on the spyglass.

Seeing it answered my question. The glass and Horn were connected.

"Try it out," Jozlyn suggested. "See what you can see."

The rocking up-and-down motion of the lobsterpod made it hard to the keep the glass steady. I poked myself in the forehead twice before bringing it to my eye.

The result was disappointing. I saw sand.

"Well?" Jozlyn asked.

I turned my head, the spyglass still fixed to my eye. Something flashed in my vision then disappeared.

"Wait!" I shouted, adjusting the position of the spyglass.

The vision returned, wiggling from left to right like a fuzzy caterpillar. Words that seemed to be written in ink

181

slowly appeared, forming a message before my eyes.

Talon Wyvern
Dragonsbane Companion

I nearly dropped the glass in excitement. "It identifies things!" I cried.

I brought the glass back to my eye, peering at Jozlyn. A new message appeared.

Enchantress Jozlyn

"It calls you an enchantress," I informed her.

Jozlyn snorted. "Of course it does."

I spun the spyglass to Josh.

Deputy Josh

read the message.

Josh swatted me playfully on the shoulder. "Stop looking at us. We already know who we are."

For the better part of an hour, we bobbed along on the lobsterpod while I studied our surroundings through the spyglass.

There was a lot to see in the Sandy Sea. Things we'd have missed without the glass. Buried treasure, mysterious places, strange creatures, and more people than I expected.

The spyglass, I discovered, even saw hidden objects.

Like shipwrecks at the bottom of the sea. It didn't matter if they were visible or buried in the sand. The spyglass found them all.

Among other things, I spied a place called Skywatch, a magical sword named Flightstrike, and the bones of a dragon. The messages sounded interesting, but seeking them out would have to be adventures for another day. We were on a quest.

My eyes were starting to hurt when a confusing message appeared. Actually, two messages. They flashed rapidly back and forth almost too fast to read.

Amalgamoth

read the first. The second was better news.

Dragonsbane Horn

The messages seemed to overlap, as if the Horn and Amalgamoth were in exactly the same spot—whatever Amalgamoth was. Maybe a person, a place, or a wizard's lost magic.

I didn't wonder long. We'd finally discovered the Horn's hiding place. That's what really mattered.

"I see it!" I cheered, pointing to our right. "This way."

Jozlyn turned the lobsterpod and we slithered speedily through the sand. The Dragonsbane Horn was close!

The Swarm

41

Aboard Rusty the lobsterpod, we slithered toward the next piece of the Horn. Captain Halfhand's Eye pointed the way. Following its trail was easy.

The Sandy Sea rolled by, and night began to fall.

As we traveled, I knew I should have felt something. Excitement, nervousness, dread—anything. But I didn't. Our quest was almost over, and I was numb.

It seemed the more I knew about the Horn and the closer we got to it, the more questions I had.

What would finding the next piece mean? Was something guarding it? Who or what was Amalgamoth?

I'd thought the end of our quest would bring answers. Instead, I was more confused than ever.

"Uh, where now?" Jozlyn muttered.

I glanced up, swatting at a swarm of insects buzzing around my head. Similar swarms had been bothering us for the last hour.

Directly ahead, a mighty cliff rose into the darkening sky. Caverns covered its face like the craters on the moon. Streams of sand trickled from them into the sea.

We'd reached the edge of the Sandy Sea. The Glittersgold Mountains towered over us like a gigantic wall. *Take the Horn, if you dare*, they seemed to challenge.

I held the spyglass to my eye and the now-familiar messages flickered back and forth when I aimed at the wall.

Amalgamoth... Dragonsbane
Horn... Amalgamoth

"There," I said, lowering the glass and pointing to a jagged cavern. "Straight ahead."

We sailed through the narrow opening into darkness, and Josh drew his sword. Insects rushed toward its light. Where were they all coming from?

The cavern formed a kind of underground river that led into the mountains. Sharp rocks stuck out from its walls and ceiling.

"I hope Amalgamoth isn't a dragon," Josh whispered. "We'll be sitting ducks in this tunnel."

Roasted ducks was more like it, but I didn't say anything. We all knew there'd be trouble if we had to fight in the tight tunnel.

Still, Josh had said what I'd been thinking. Amalgamoth

185

could be a dragon. Shelolth was a dragon and she wanted the Horn. Another dragon could want it, too.

Kheeeeeeh!

Suddenly the lobsterpod lurched upward, hissing angrily. Its front claws snapped at the air. Josh lost his balance and slipped from its back.

"*Ungh!*" he grunted, landing with a surprising thud. The sand was only a few inches deep!

"Looks like we have to walk from here," he said. He climbed to his feet and carefully scooted past the agitated lobsterpod.

"Poor Rusty," Jozlyn cooed, patting the creature gently like it was a family dog.

I rolled my eyes, thankful for the darkness so she couldn't see me.

We managed to climb down without getting pinched and set off on foot. The lobsterpod hissed once more then retreated down the tunnel.

Josh led the way, his sword lighting our path. I came last with Talon perched on my arm. The tunnel twisted crazily, turning this way and that. If not for the fact that it sloped steadily downward, I could never have found my way out.

Fff-zzzzzzzt!

A low buzzing sound tickled my ears and made the hairs on the back of my neck stand out.

"Stop!" I hissed. "Did you hear that?"

Josh and Jozlyn froze, listening. Talon cocked her head.

Fff-zzzzzzzzt! The noise came again, not quite as low.

—Wings. Many wings.— Talon warned.

Hearing that, I didn't hesitate. "Run!" I yelled. Jozlyn and Josh might not have heard the sound, but my ears were never wrong.

Jozlyn started to turn and I snatched her arm. "Not that way! Something's behind us!"

Her eyes widened in understanding and she took off at a sprint. Josh and I charged after her.

Our feet pounded the ground. Our heavy breathing echoed down the tunnel. The wings buzzed louder. *Fff-zzzzzzzzt!*

Jozlyn rounded a sharp corner, and I glanced over my shoulder. In the flickering light of Josh's sword, I saw them. The swarm.

Thousands of insects writhed and slithered behind me in a dark cloud. They coated the walls and floor of the tunnel like paint sloshing through a tube.

Some had stingers and pinchers. Others had hundreds of legs and huge, velvety wings. Their *chitter-clack-scratch-click* made my skin crawl.

I shrieked and shoved Josh hard in the back. Together we shot around the corner and saw the trap too late.

A huge cavern opened before us. The ceiling vanished into darkness and the floor dropped like a pit. Oily grey webbing crisscrossed the pit in a tangled net.

Running too fast to stop, we fell.

Amalgamoth

42

Sploingk!

I tumbled into the webbing, bounced once, then froze. A gluey substance coated my legs, arms, and back like I was a fly in a spider's lair.

Josh crashed next to me and lost his grip on his sword. The fire on the blade flickered weakly then died.

Buzzing deafeningly, the swarm sped into the cavern behind us. In a cloud of darkness, the insects darted about as if looking for something…or someone.

Amalgamoth, I knew without doubt.

"Look out!" Jozlyn screamed. Lying flat on my back, I couldn't see her.

From the blackness overhead came a taunting chuckle that sounded like a hundred rattlesnakes shaking their tails. "Z*zz*omething ha*zz* fallen into our ne*zzz*t," the chilling voice hissed.

I squinted into the gloom and saw a monstrous shape rapidly descending. Huge fly-like eyes as big as my head blinked slowly.

They belonged to a nightmare.

A bloated insect the size of a dragon lowered itself down a silken, rope-like strand. The monster had the body of a praying mantis, the wings of a moth, and the tail of a scorpion.

Someone shrieked and I joined in.

Amalgamoth swiveled its head, peering at me from an odd angle. "Z*zzt*-welcome Dragon*zzz*bane," it buzzed, a stream of mucus leaking from between the mandibles on its mouth.

As I met Amalgamoth's awful gaze, the insect swarm landed on the monster and started to crawl and burrow into its body. Amalgamoth swelled, growing larger.

My stomach churned in disgust. Amalgamoth wasn't one big insect. It was thousands and thousands of them, all creeping and wiggling on top of each other.

"We thank you, *zzzt*," Amalgamoth gloated, "for bringing u*zzz* more of the Horn." The monster's face twisted into a look that could only be called an evil smile.

"Buzz off!" Jozlyn snarled defiantly.

Amalgamoth calmly released its rope and flapped its moth wings, gliding to my left. I heard Jozlyn scream then go terrifyingly silent.

"Leave her alone!" Josh roared, struggling helplessly in

the web. "Fight me!"

He was brave, all right, but bravery wasn't going to be enough. He needed his sword. Its flames could burn….

—Tell him to be ready.—

Talon's sudden words startled me. I'd forgotten she could read my mind and that she wasn't stuck in the web.

Screeching her war cry, Talon soared from the tunnel. Even in the darkness, her metallic wings glinted like an oiled sword blade.

"Josh," I gasped, "your sword!" It wasn't much of a warning, and I prayed he understood.

Talon snatched the weapon and yanked it from the webbing, her wings straining. The blade came free with a gooey *squipp!* just as Amalgamoth turned.

"What'*zzz* thi*zzz*?" it buzzed in surprise.

The brief delay was all the time Talon needed. She dropped the sword into Josh's hand, and blue flames came to life. The webbing near Josh evaporated, and the glue around him started to melt.

Grunting with effort, Josh struggled to his feet. Strands of glue clung to his back like the strings on a puppet, and the web swayed dangerously under him.

If much more of the web burned, we'd all fall.

"This is a flyswatter with your name on it!" Josh bellowed. He glared at Amalgamoth with his sword aimed directly at the monster.

This time Amalgamoth didn't respond. It attacked. With

a shriek and the speed of a striking snake, it scuttled across the web.

Josh held his ground until the very last moment. Just before Amalgamoth struck, he dove over me and slashed his sword again and again into the webbing. His arms hacked and chopped like a woodcutter swinging a hatchet.

Flames flashed and glue sizzled under his blows. The web trembled, disintegrating rapidly.

Then suddenly something popped and the whole web came free. It groaned and creaked like the floorboards in a haunted house.

Amalgamoth shrieked again. Talon squawked and Jozlyn screamed. The web split apart, collapsing on itself.

"Not again!" I gasped as we fell.

This Quest is About You

43

Wet sand broke my fall. Good thing, but I was so sick of sand.

Jozlyn and Josh landed next, followed by the tremendous thud of Amalgamoth. The monster buzzed in rage.

"Everyone alright?" I asked quickly. Of course I wasn't talking to Amalgamoth.

"*Y*-yeah," Jozlyn replied shakily. In the dim light I saw her climb to her feet. "But *w*-where are you? I can't see."

I'd forgotten again that only I could see in the dark.

"I'm right here," I said, but my attention turned to Josh. He hadn't moved or made a sound, and the flames on his sword had gone out. If I could reach it….

Amalgamoth's buzzing chuckle stung my ears. "We are all ju*zzzt* fine, thank you."

From across the cavern, out eyes met, and I froze. Amalgamoth knew what I was thinking. It knew I wanted the sword.

Terror filled my mind. *What am I doing here?* I wailed silently. *I'm no warrior! There's a monster trying to kill me!*

All of my old fears rushed back in an instant. My fears of failure and my self-doubt. I was too young to be on a quest. I needed babysitters.

My legs trembled and my knees started to buckle. Amalgamoth would grind me into the sand and take my piece of the Horn as easily as it would rob a sleeping infant of a bottle.

I wasn't a hero. What had I been thinking?

—You are the Dragonsbane. This quest is about you.—

So lost in my fears, I didn't recognize Talon's voice right away. I watched Amalgamoth stalk slowly across the sand, eyes flicking between me and Josh's fallen sword.

—This quest is about you.—

Talon repeated the words calmly, patiently. *Remember who you are*, they seemed to whisper. *Remember the Dragonsbane.*

Thunder roared in my ears, the sound of the Horn. I heard it clearly as if I were blowing it.

The sound reminded me of who I was, and I came awake inside. Confidence and determination swelled in my heart. I was Jasiah Dragonsbane. This quest was about me. It was mine.

And so was the Horn.

Without taking my eyes from Amalgamoth, I leaped. My hand grasped the hilt of Josh's sword, and I bounded from my knees to my feet in a blink.

"The Horn is mine," I roared as much to myself as at Amalgamoth. "All of it. Where is the next piece?"

Amalgamoth reared back like a stallion, screeching and buzzing. Its wings flapped powerfully, whipping up funnels of sand.

There, buried beneath the swarms of creeping-crawling insects in Amalgamoth's chest, I saw the second piece of the Dragonsbane Horn.

Thousands of insects nested on it like maggots in a garbage heap, feeding and drawing from its power.

The sight was revolting. The Horn should never have been used like that. Amalgamoth needed to be destroyed.

We attacked at the same time. Amalgamoth rumbled toward me, its scorpion's tail slashing. I brought up Josh's sword, aiming at nothing in particular, just hoping to connect.

Zzzzzzzzt!

A sizzling buzz reverberated throughout the cavern. The noise might have been the flames on the sword. It might have been Amalgamoth.

Pain exploded in my left calf and I collapsed, rolling onto my back. Amalgamoth's bloated shape shrieked and blazed above me.

We'd both scored a hit!

Flames writhed on one of Amalgamoth's wings, sending insects scurrying to escape the blaze. They buzzed the air, burrowed into the sand, and pelted me like hail in a storm. The wing drifted apart like a cloud caught in a breeze.

There was hope! Amalgamoth wasn't invincible.

I tried to drag myself backward, desperate to get to my feet. But my wounded leg wouldn't cooperate. It felt like lead and wouldn't move at all.

The sting from Amalgamoth's tail had paralyzed me! The pain in my leg was gone and a tingling sensation was spreading quickly into my thigh.

One word echoed in my mind. *Poison!*

Amalgamoth saw me struggling and chuckled triumphantly. "Now your pie*zzz* of the Horn i*zzz* our*zzz*."

44

We'd failed our quest and Amalgamoth had won. Soon the monster would have both pieces of the Dragonsbane Horn.

"Get up!" Jozlyn screeched.

During the battle, I'd forgotten she was there. Not that it mattered much. It was too late for me. The poison was spreading, and soon I wouldn't be able to move at all.

"Run," I gasped hoarsely. "*P*-poison…." I couldn't say anymore. The poison was weakening me, and my eyelids drooped heavily.

Amalgamoth shifted its bug eyes from me to Jozlyn. "*Zzzt*-be gone with you, witch-girl. Tell the world to fear Amalgamoth."

Surprised, I found the strength to turn my head. How had Amalgamoth known Jozlyn was a witch?

"Enchantress," Jozlyn said coldly. She stomped through

the sand toward us, clutching her tiny broom like a stake intended for a vampire. She didn't slow as she recited a spell.

Out, out!
Hear me shout.
Poison now obey.

Route doubt—
Turn about.
Pick me, come this way.

She shouted the words, just like her spell said. When she finished, she heaved her broom across the cavern at me. I was unable to move as I watched it strike my elbow.

Tingling warmth shot through me, and Jozlyn took a ragged breath, her skin turned blue. Then her eyes rolled into her head and she collapsed to the ground.

"Jozlyn!" I cried, scrambling to my hands and knees without thinking. The pain in my calf returned, burning like I'd bumped it against a hot stove.

I sucked in a sharp breath.

I could feel my leg! I could move! Jozlyn's spell had taken the poison from me and put it into her.

"*Zzzt!* Clever magic but too late!" Amalgamoth buzzed.

I wheeled in time to see the insect charging. Josh's sword had tumbled from my hand, so I threw handfuls of sand into Amalgamoth's face. I had no other weapon.

Amalgamoth lashed out its tail like a whip, and I dove right, rolling, ignoring the clumps of sand that sprayed into the air. The tail struck again and again, sending up more sandy explosions.

All I could do was jump and roll, barely ahead of the attacks. Amalgamoth was incredibly fast. One wrong move and it would be over.

My chest heaved for breath. My leg throbbed. My eyes watered and itched from the flying sand.

Blindly, I stumbled forward until something solid caught my foot and dragged me down.

Josh's sword! The one thing that could save me had doomed me.

A fuzzy insect leg batted my head and sent me skidding across the ground. I squeezed my eyes shut to clear them and opened them in time to see—

Death.

Amalgamoth loomed directly above me. It raised one leg and stabbed it through my sleeve and into the sand, pinning me to the ground. Its tail dipped with cruel slowness. Poison glistened on its tip.

—The Horn!— Talon squawked urgently in my head.

What? With my arm pinned against my side, I couldn't reach my belt. But when Amalgamoth shifted to deliver the perfect blow, metal and ivory glinted in its chest.

The second piece of the Horn!

I threw out my hand without thinking, clawing for the

Horn. Insects swarmed over my skin, biting and stinging. The pain was almost unbearable.

When my fingers clutched the Horn, Amalgamoth wailed pitifully. Its breath blasted me with a stench of sickeningly sweet honey. Bugs tumbled into my face, and my arm felt like it was on fire.

"*Zzzzzt! Nooo!*" Amalgamoth howled. Its fly eyes focused on me with a desperate look.

I stared back without sympathy. "I am the Dragonsbane," I snarled, "and this belongs to me!"

Then I ripped the Horn free.

Amalgamoth exploded instantly into a million buzzing bugs and was gone. No longer swarming, the insects ricocheted off one another, bouncing against me, the sand, and into the air.

I clutched the Horn to my chest and rolled onto my stomach with my eyes closed. The buzzing echoed in the cavern for an eternity.

Finally, the noise faded and I sat up gingerly. My body ached from everywhere at once, itching with bug bites and throbbing with bruises. I was exhausted.

But I had one thing left to do.

Moving slowly, I unhooked my piece of the Horn and fitted it against Amalgamoth's. The pieces snapped together easily and became one. No line remained to show that they had ever been separated.

I took a deep breath, raised the Horn, and blew.

Silvermight Found

45

The second time I blew the Horn was nothing like the first. I didn't feel anything special inside. I didn't learn the secret to any mystery.

Instead, the world crackled with electricity.

The Horn's trumpeting blast revived Josh and Jozlyn, and with Amalgamoth defeated, the poison evaporated from Jozlyn's body.

"What happened?" Josh asked, scooping his sword from the sand.

"No, what's *happening*?" Jozlyn corrected.

The sand in the cavern swelled suddenly, sloshing and rising like a wave. Wind howled and knocked us off our feet.

"Hang on!" I wailed as the sand heaved and rolled forward. Building up steam, it scooped us up like a raft adrift on a wild river.

Caught in the current, we shot out of the cavern and into the tunnel. Sand churned noisily behind us. Rocks and stone flashed by dangerously close.

What had I done? I'd expected something good to happen when I blew the Horn. I hadn't expected an earthquake.

We exploded from the tunnel and crashed to the surprisingly rocky ground beyond. Sand swirled violently in the air, clouding the sky and painting the world brown, silver, and gold. Little remained on the ground.

What had happened to the Sandy Sea?

The sand rained down like blinding snow, piling high in odd shapes. It formed jagged pyramids and squat lumps. It was going to bury us alive.

On our hands and knees, we clutched each other and waited for the world to end. Hours passed before we dared to move or even open our eyes. When we did, we discovered the word had been remade.

The Sandy Sea was gone. Mountains spiraled into the sky where the sea had been. Shining fortresses and gleaming buildings dotted the landscape. Roads of solid silver snaked here and there.

"Where are we?" Josh mumbled, clearly amazed.

Except for the buildings and roads, it looked like we were somewhere in the Glittersgold Mountains. But that was impossible. This was supposed to be the Sandy Sea.

Jozlyn shook her head. "No, Josh, that's the wrong

question. You should ask, where did everything come from?"

Her question answered everything for me. "The sand," I whispered. "It was in the sand. That's what happened to Silvermight."

Without a doubt, I knew the riddle of lost Silvermight. It hadn't disappeared and it hadn't gone anywhere.

It had crumbled to sand when Amalgamoth stole the Horn.

Krrzzzzt-THOOOM!

In a brilliant flash, Medium Mirelda's gaudy wagon suddenly appeared on the silver road in front of us. Its swinging doors whisked open, and the slender fortune-teller winked at us from inside.

"Many congratulations," she smiled, "but no fortune today. Please make your coming inside now."

Too surprised to ask questions, we climbed aboard. Amazingly, the sight inside surprised us more.

Seated behind Mirelda's tiny table were Uncle Arick, Kadze, and Wizard Ast. The three of them watched us enter with smiles on their faces.

"Uncle Arick!" I exclaimed, almost diving over the table. "You're alright—and Kadze, too!" Tears welled in my eyes. I'd been so afraid for them!

"Of course we are," my uncle boomed happily. "One pack of shaddim isn't enough to defeat a Dragonsbane." He winked at me knowingly.

"*Not even the worst of storms brings every leaf from the tree*," Kadze added, quoting one of his famous proverbs.

I smiled at him, too excited to bother with figuring out what he'd meant.

Wizard Ast interrupted by springing lightly out of his chair. "We are all very proud-pleased indeed," he beamed. His long beard and mustache were white with age, but his eyes sparkled merrily. "You three have shown-demonstrated remarkable courage."

Jozlyn, Josh, and I opened out mouths to thank him, but a piercing squawk drowned out our words.

Skrawt!

In a blur of blinding colors, Talon soared unexpectedly into the wagon and landed on my gauntlet.

Uncle Arick nodded approvingly, and Wizard Ast cleared his throat. "You *four*," the wizard amended, glancing at the wyvern. "Pardon-excuse me."

—He can be trained, too.— Talon joked with me privately.

"But now, we must return-head back to Tiller's Field," Wizard Ast continued. "Young Jozlyn and Josh have responsibilities, and Jasiah's new companions-comrades await him."

I gasped and heard Josh and Jozlyn do the same. *New companions?* That meant my friends wouldn't be going with me to find the third piece of the Horn!

Wizard Ast said no more. He nodded to Medium

Mirelda, and the fortune-teller spun her magic globe. When her finger punched down on Tiller's Field, the wagon lurched into motion.

My quest for the Dragonsbane Horn was about to begin— again.

The End

This Knightscares Adventure Continues in Book #2

The Dragonsbane Horn: Trek Through Tangleroot

Knightscares Adventures

#1: Cauldron Cooker's Night
#2: Skull in the Birdcage
#3: Early Winter's Orb

The Dragonsbane Horn Trilogy

#1: Voyage to Silvermight
#2: Trek Through Tangleroot *(Coming Soon)*
#3: Hunt for Hollowdeep *(Coming Soon)*

Want Free Knightscares ?

Join the Official Knightscares Fan Club Today!

Visit www.knightscares.com

Read the latest conjurings, spells, and news from the co-wizards, David and Charlie.

Join the Free Fan Club
Get Your "Name in Lights"
Preview Upcoming Adventures
Invite the Authors to Your School
Meet the Writers
Lots More!

Knightscares Artwork Winners

Both artists will receive a free autographed copy of The Dragonsbane Horn: Voyage to Silvermight.

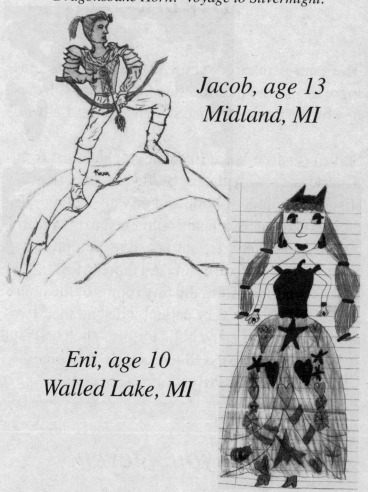

Jacob, age 13
Midland, MI

Eni, age 10
Walled Lake, MI

Great Work! Thank You!

Voyage to Silvermight Artwork

The hand-painted cover art, official Knightscares logo, maps, and interior illustrations were all created by the talented artist Steven Spenser Ledford.

Steven is a free-lance fine and graphic artist from Charleston, SC with nearly 20 years experience. His work includes public and private wall murals, comic book pencil, ink and color, magazine illustrations and cover art, t-shirt designs, sculptures, portraits, painted furniture and more. Most of his work is produced from the tiny rooms of the house he shares with his very patient wife and their two children—Xena (a psychotic tortoise-shell cat) and Emma (a Jack Russell terrier). He welcomes inquiries at PtByNmbrs@aol.com.

Thank you, Steven!